"Why did you have to kiss me?"

Even as she asked him, Julia felt he was mocking her.

But Guy only smiled indifferently. "Surely for some things there doesn't always have to be a reason? In this case, for instance, don't you think a reason might sound too much like an excuse? Blame the circumstances if you must. The isolation and heat of the day, or merely impulse."

"Impulse?"

His smile became even more cynical. "You're a lovely girl, Julia. Perhaps I was caught unawares and you tempted me."

"You've too much control."

"Yes. Yet—" his eyes grew shades colder "—I don't believe anyone is infallible. At least I don't now. Maybe unconsciously, when I held you and kissed you, I was trying to deal with the restraint that you often wear like an armor."

Books by Margaret Pargeter

HARLEQUIN PRESENTS

HARLEQUIN ROMANCES

These books may be available at your local bookseller.

For a free catalog listing all titles currently available,
send your name and address to:

Harlequin Reader Service
P.O. Box 52040, Phoenix, AZ   85072-9988
Canadian address: Stratford, Ontario   N5A 6W2

MARGARET PARGETER

storm in the night

Harlequin Books

TORONTO • NEW YORK • LONDON
AMSTERDAM • PARIS • SYDNEY • HAMBURG
STOCKHOLM • ATHENS • TOKYO • MILAN

Harlequin Presents first edition January 1984
ISBN 0-373-10660-2

Original hardcover edition published in 1983
by Mills & Boon Limited

CHAPTER ONE

JULIA Ward stared at the tall, dark-haired Frenchman whose dominating presence filled her with feelings of mutiny and awe. Even before she opened the door to him she had sensed his authority from the way he had knocked. His cold blue eyes had flicked over her, and, after ascertaining she was the girl he was looking for, he introduced himself briefly as Guy Guerard. Walking past her, without waiting to be invited in, he had entered her one-roomed flat, and from a vantage point beside the window, where the light fell on Julia's face and not his, he viewed both her and the room disparagingly.

'Close the door, *mademoiselle*.'

He spoke curtly and Julia obeyed, closing her mouth as well, flushing to realise she probably resembled a stranded fish. She knew who Guy Guerard was, although this was the first time she had met him. Her mother's sister had married a widower with a seven-year-old son about thirty years ago. The man before her was obviously this son, and, despite herself, Julia shivered. Christine Ward, her mother, had been French and when she married an Englishman her family had disapproved and disowned her, but occasionally she had talked of the Camargue, a place of wild bulls and horses and even wilder men!

Yves Guerard, like Julia's parents, was now dead, but Julia wondered if he had been anything like his son. Guy Guerard, with his faultless English and elegantly tailored suit, resembled a sophisticated city-dweller more than a Camargue cowboy, owning countless rough acres, but, as her glance explored his square-jawed features, Julia drew a sharp breath. What he was doing here she had no idea, but she suddenly wished she had endeavoured to answer her aunt's last letter.

As if his thoughts were on the same thing, Guy Guerard broke the rather fraught silence to ask abruptly, 'Mavis wrote. Why didn't you reply?'

'I haven't been well.'

Frosty eyes rested on Julia's pale cheeks. He didn't appear to consider her excuse good enough. 'It might have saved me a journey if you had. You must have realised she would worry about you. She has been deeply upset since you lost your parents and she is no longer young, *mademoiselle*.'

Julia flushed unhappily. He was only repeating what her aunt had already said, but she'd had such a bad dose of 'flu that even to get out of bed had been a struggle. And, although she had recovered, she still didn't seem to have the energy to do more than was absolutely necessary. Resentfully she felt the impact of Guy Guerard's powerful vitality, doubting that he had ever known what it was like to feel deprived of strength.

'I'm sorry,' she murmured, realising it might be futile trying to make him understand.

His voice hardened imperceptibly. 'She has asked you to come to France to live.'

Julia nodded reluctantly. 'It was very kind of her.'

'I agree,' he regarded her with cool austerity, 'So, *mademoiselle*, you'd better pack your bags and prepare to leave with me. At once!'

Julia's grey eyes darkened with startled bewilderment. She couldn't take him seriously, but she felt so faint she had to sit down. She had thought her legs were growing stronger and was dismayed to find them still weak.

'I—I couldn't do that, *monsieur*,' she protested, 'Even if I did want to accept my aunt's invitation, you couldn't expect me to leave straight away. I'd have things to see to, to cancel. I just can't walk out.'

'No, of course not,' he allowed coldly. 'I'll give you an hour, *mademoiselle*.'

Julia's breath caught on an incredulous gasp. With a sinking feeling in her breast, she stared at the uncompromising jawline, the hard, straight mouth. From the way he swept her protests aside he had obviously no intention of listening. He had the air of a man with a duty to perform and no inclination to waste time over it! She forced herself to speak calmly while unconsciously fighting his forceful personality.

'Please be reasonable, *monsieur*. If I decide to go to France, I can find my own way there. There's no need for you to bother with me. It's not as though I haven't travelled before.'

'Only with your parents, I imagine.'

'No,' Julia blinked. 'I used to join them for school holidays, when they were usually abroad, and I frequently travelled by myself.'

'*Mon Dieu!*' he muttered under his breath, as though he found this reprehensible, 'From now on, whenever you wish to go anywhere you must consult me.'

As he gazed at her grimly, Julia suddenly guessed that he had authorised her aunt's invitation, that no one did anything on his estate without his full permission. In parts of France, her mother had told her, the old feudal system still existed. In spite of Guy Guerard's civilised appearance, he might be quite the opposite underneath. Instinct warned her that if she went with him she might never escape.

Uneasily she stirred as he continued in the same vein. 'Apparently your parents were at fault over many things, but fortunately it is not too late. You aren't yet twenty. Once you are living in my house, I will do my best to redress the balance.'

'Re—what did you say, *monsieur*?'

He contemplated her severely. 'You heard, *mademoiselle*. You appear to be of average intelligence. In France we will begin your education again.'

She still didn't know what he meant, but she was sure

she didn't like the sound of it. It certainly didn't make her keener to go with him.

'I don't wish to live in your house, *monsieur*,' she replied, her voice rising defiantly, 'and you can't make me!'

'You can't live here,' he retorted implacably. 'London's no place for a young girl on her own, existing in one disreputable room, without a job or money.'

Drawing a furious breath, Julia asked sharply, 'How do you know these things?'

'I had you thoroughly investigated.'

'It's not possible!' she whispered incredulously.

He smiled slightly. She caught a glimpse of strong white teeth but no amusement. 'Anything is possible,' he snapped, then, with a little more patience. 'I'd appreciate it, *mademoiselle*, if you would kindly stop arguing and do as you're told. Your aunt is naturally deeply concerned. I am here to take you to her, but I had to make sure first that there was nothing about you which would add to rather than alleviate her distress.'

Julia looked at him, aware of despair sweeping over her. What defence had she against this man whose actions she suspected might be as decisive as his words? 'You can't make me,' she repeated stubbornly.

He eyed her cynically. 'Your landlady informs me you owe her rent.'

She hadn't seen her landlady for two weeks. Mrs Lund had called, but Julia had been too ill to go to the door. She wouldn't tell Guy Guerard this, though, as if he knew how ill she had been it might only provide him with a further excuse to assert his authority.

'You had no business discussing me with her!' she retorted angrily.

His impatience returned. 'You are family, Julia. I consider you are my business.'

'I can't be family to you,' Julia contradicted swiftly.

'There's no real blood relationship between you and my aunt. I mean, she's only your stepmother.'

'If she wasn't my mother,' he answered coldly, 'Mavis was my father's wife, which in no way rules out my obligations. Nor mine to you,' he added firmly. After a moment, as if giving her time to digest this, he said suavely, 'In France, if you are obedient and prove amenable, I will provide you with a *dot* large enough to enable you to make a good marriage.'

Julia's mouth opened helplessly as he watched her coolly. 'A—*dot*? That's a dowry, isn't it?'

'Of course,' his dark brows lifted carelessly. 'Without one you might never manage to find a husband of any standing.'

'I presume,' Julia almost spluttered, 'You will supply a husband as well?'

'Naturally.'

Julia was stunned, and while she knew she might be wiser to drop the subject, she felt she couldn't leave it there. 'What,' she countered fiercely, 'if I don't want to be married?'

His mouth curled derisively. 'All women do. And, *mademoiselle*, I don't intend keeping you for ever.' Coolly his eyes swept over her. 'A little more flesh on your bones – in places. Some healthier colour in your cheeks and your pink-and-white fairness might prove well nigh irresistible.'

But not to him! Yet, as their eyes met, Julia had a feeling that he was seeing her for the first time as a woman. His dark, probing gaze seemed to stir within her something she had never been conscious of before—she could actually feel her nerve ends beginning to tingle. Because of this she was thrown into a state of confusion, which increased when she heard herself utter irrationally. 'I've had no experience.'

'You don't expect me to supply this also?' he laughed.

As she went scarlet to the roots of her hair, his

laughter faded, but she sensed he was still amused. 'I suppose, as my cousin, you feel free to speak frankly?' she muttered coldly.

'I'm not your cousin, *mademoiselle*.'

Julia frowned. 'I thought you regarded yourself as my cousin, from what you said, and as you're taking such an interest in my affairs.'

'Julia!' he muttered impatiently. 'I am doing this for your aunt's sake, no other reason. Now, are you going to be sensible and pack your clothes, or do you want me to do it for you?'

Suddenly Julia gave in. Truth to tell, she had little strength left to fight him. Her brief surge of energy had faded, leaving her weak to the point of tears. A visit to France might be nice and her mother would have wanted her to go. And, despite what Guy Guerard had said, she needn't stay long. Not for a moment did she believe her aunt would want her there permanently. After all, she had a daughter of her own.

By evening they were in Paris. Julia, who had never been there before, gazed about her in wonder as they drove from the airport. Her mother had always been reluctant to return to France and her father had never tried to make her change her mind. He had frequently declared he hated it because of what his wife's family had done to her.

They hadn't gone straight to Provence as Guy Guerard had a business meeting in the capital in the morning. He instructed the cab to take them to a well known hotel, where he had a suite reserved.

'We will fly south later tomorrow,' he said.

The hustle of their departure had taken more out of Julia than she cared to admit, but it wasn't until they reached the hotel that she collapsed. She didn't remember fainting in the lounge of the suite he had reserved; she knew nothing until she woke up and found herself in bed.

Her eyes widened in confused astonishment as she

saw Guy Guerard standing over her, a glass in his hand. 'Drink this,' he commanded curtly, sitting down beside her, holding the brandy to her lips.

Julia closed her eyes tightly before opening them again, to make sure she wasn't dreaming, but he was still there. Weakly obedient, she sat up, only to discover, to her startled surprise, that her shoulders were bare.

'Where are my clothes?' she cried, clutching a sheet about her.

'Don't worry, I haven't pawned them,' he replied dryly. 'They're over there.'

Was he being deliberately obtuse? Her eyes flew to a nearby chair over which was draped her skirt and blouse. Weakly she glared at him. 'Who took them off?'

'I did,' he confessed unrepentantly. 'What else would you expect me to do?'

Julia wasn't sure. She wished her pulses would stop fluttering so wildly at the thought of his hard hands on her body. Even to think of it made her tremble.

'I don't know,' she whispered, subsiding.

His mouth thinned as he regarded her heightening colour. 'Did you imagine I was trying to take advantage of you, Julia?'

'No.' She bent her head, attempting to conceal her embarrassment. How often had her father expounded that Frenchmen were lecherous! She never remembered taking much notice of him, but his words must have made a greater impression than she had realised. 'I'm sorry,' she mumbled, as Guy Guerard appeared to be waiting for an apology.

She sensed his resigned shrug. 'You should have told me how ill you had been, Julia.'

'How did you guess?'

'I'd be a fool not to realise your thinness isn't normal. You're all bones and blue veins.'

'It was only 'flu.'

'Influenza?' he nodded grimly. 'That tallies. Who looked after you? Not your dragon of a landlady?'

'There was no one,' Julia tried to be honest. 'I don't think Mrs Lund knew I was ill.'

He sighed. 'Which might also explain why you are so reluctant to let me help you now. You're like a small, prickly hedgehog, my child, but one can be too independent.'

'I suppose so,' she agreed ruefully, forgetting to protest as he slipped a firm but gentle arm around her, to lift her towards the glass he still held. More submissive than she could ever remember being before with anyone, she rested against him, drinking the brandy, allowing him to hold her while the fiery liquid coursed through her veins.

'Better?'

She nodded as he set the glass aside and began carefully massaging the back of her neck. The movement of his hands over her skin was soothing, she could almost feel the tense muscles in her shoulders relax and she snuggled into him with a grateful smile. Feelings of drowsiness were fighting with a less definable emotion when he stopped.

Feeling curiously deprived, she just managed to restrain a word of protest when he laid her back against her pillows. She wondered why his mouth tightened as he moved away from her.

'Are you hungry?' he asked, with surprising sharpness, considering how gentle his hands had been.

'I'm not sure,' she replied truthfully.

'You refused to eat on the plane. Have you had anything all day?'

His cool questions stung, but she merely shook her head.

'That's probably why you fainted,' he said curtly, impatience returning to his dark blue eyes. 'After you've had a rest, I'll have your dinner sent up. I'm hoping, by tomorrow you'll be recovered enough to travel.'

'I will be,' she assured him quickly. 'I don't want to be a nuisance.'

He shrugged. 'My life is frequently cluttered with problems I'd rather be without, *mademoiselle*. One gets used to it, and I don't regard them all as a nuisance.'

Julia knew she should be feeling resentful rather than anxious as he continued watching her broodingly, but somehow her former antagonism had faded. 'Are you going out?' she enquired humbly, having no wish to spoil his evening.

He turned away. 'I may go down to the restaurant to eat, but otherwise I will be working. I'll be in the lounge if you need me.'

The telephone rang as he went through the door and he didn't bother to close it. Julia heard him pick up the receiver and, after a moment heard him exclaim, *'Ah, bonsoir, ma chérie! Comment vas-tu?'*

Julia spoke excellent French, and she wondered if Guy Guerard realised. He was obviously speaking to a lady and sounded surprised, but as his tones became more rapid she had difficulty in following him. It must be someone who was familiar with his whereabouts, or she wouldn't have rung him here. He had said he was staying in, but perhaps this lady would persuade him to change his mind.

She was half prepared for the faint expression of satisfaction on his face when he came back to her. 'That was an old friend,' he explained unnecessarily. 'I'm afraid I shall be going out after all, *mademoiselle*.'

After he had departed, resplendent, Julia thought, in a white jacket, she sat patiently in the lounge waiting for her dinner to arrive. She felt lonely after he had gone, but she couldn't really complain as he hadn't been unconcerned. He had refused to leave until she was safely bathed and ensconced in a comfortable chair, wearing a warm dressing-gown. He had asked her not to lock the bathroom door and she had obeyed him meekly when he had forbidden her to linger in the shower. He had even insisted on making sure she had dried her hair properly, by running his hand lightly over it.

'You may think I fuss too much, Julia,' he had fixed a stern eye on her as she had glanced at him wonderingly, 'but it is clear to me that you need looking after.'

Julia had hesitated before admitting softly, 'It does give me a nice feeling. I've always wished I'd been able to see more of my father.'

For a moment he had stared sharply when she said that. Somehow, she gained the impression that she had startled him. Then he had said firmly, 'I am full of good parental advice, as you are already discovering, *mademoiselle*. I've certainly had enough experience.'

It didn't strike Julia until he had gone that this must mean he was married. It amazed her that she hadn't thought of this before. If he wasn't, there were other possibilities. He could be divorced or separated from his wife—and there must be children. She tried to imagine what his children would be like. His sons would be tall and dark, younger images of himself, with something of their father's strength already stamped on their youthful features.

The more Julia pondered over it, the more she became convinced Guy Guerard had a wife somewhere. And his apparent resolve to find her a good husband seemed to confirm this. Even if he was having difficulties himself, he must still consider marriage an estimable estate or he wouldn't be so keen to push others into it!

When her dinner arrived, served by two extremely correct waiters, she felt almost too depressed to eat. She might have left it if it hadn't occurred to her that if she did she might be too weak to leave the next day and Guy Guerard would be angry. With increasing determination she tackled her soup and tried to stop wondering if his wife was very beautiful.

She attempted to concentrate instead on the problems facing her. If only she had trained for a career, how much easier everything might have been. She could live with the Guerards for a while, but she had no intention of being thrust into a marriage she didn't want or of being persuaded to remain in France for ever. It wasn't her environment and she didn't believe she could settle permanently in a foreign land among strange people. The future might look grim, but it had to be faced. It wouldn't do to dwell constantly on the present—or in the past.

She hadn't got her parents any more. 'Full stop!' she muttered aloud, pushing aside her soup as a tear fell into it. They had never bought a house in England as they had been so seldom there. They had never had a proper home anywhere as they had never been long in one place. They had intended living in England when her father, a geologist, retired. Julia had often listened to them, making plans which could now never come to fruition. After she left school they had sent money for her to find a room and told her to look for a job, without apparently wondering how she was going to find one, ill equipped as she was. She had been fortunate in finding a room, but it wouldn't be there when she returned. Guy Guerard had cancelled it, and while she still felt indignant at his high-handedness, she couldn't honestly be sorry she hadn't to go back to that particular place.

As the sun was shining the following morning, Julia felt her spirits rising. After a good breakfast and a stroll with Guy along a pleasant boulevard, she felt strong enough to accompany him to the airport, later in the day. Already she found herself thinking of him as Guy, although she was careful to still address him as Monsieur. He had helped her to repack and she had continued to be surprised by the efficiency of his movements, the swiftness with which he got things done. Everything he did appeared to be coolly thought out and accomplished with lightning speed, so as not to waste a moment. She couldn't help wondering if his whole life was ruled by such intelligent, deliberate action, or if he ever did anything on impulse.

The evening before, he had knocked on her door, on returning to the hotel, and found her awake. It had only been a few minutes after eleven, but when he had seen that she wasn't asleep, he had ordered hot milk, which, when it arrived, he had laced with another good measure of brandy. This time he hadn't held her as she drank it, but he had sat casually on the edge of her bed to make sure she did. Afterwards she had had difficulty in keeping her eyes open, but she suspected that was due as much to his reassuring presence as to the effects of the brandy, but when she had tried to thank him he had merely drawled sardonically, 'Only what a father would have done, *mademoiselle.*'

He appeared to be still in a good mood this morning but it wasn't until they were driving from the airport at Marseilles, en route to their final destination, that Julia plucked up enough courage to ask about his wife.

'I am not married, Julia.' He drove a powerful Ferrari and looked straight ahead.

Because he didn't ask why she had imagined he was, she felt rather confounded. She could judge nothing from his silence, but it wasn't exactly encouraging. He had answered her question, but had obviously no intention of satisfying her curiosity as to why he was still a bachelor at his time of life. She hoped he would never guess how much time she had given over to wondering what his wife was like. Then the strange stirrings of relief she had known when he had confessed to still being single, faded quickly as another thought struck her.

'You are perhaps engaged, *monsieur*?'

'Engaged? Ah, you mean, affianced?' a dark brow rose against a chiselled profile, 'No, I am not that either, *mademoiselle*. Not yet.'

'I—see.'

His mouth quirked wryly as he shot a glance at her

doubtful face. 'What is it you see, Julia? I suspect your imagination is behind all this doubtful speculation? Wouldn't it be better if you thought of something else?'

'Perhaps you're right.' A faint colour stole into Julia's cheeks as she forced herself to confess, 'Since I heard you talking to someone on the telephone, last night, I admit I've been curious.'

He replied almost idly. 'There's bound to be much in your new life which will arouse your curiosity, but I'd advise you to take it in easy stages, *ma chère*, otherwise you might get a kind of mental indigestion.'

That he called her *ma chère* seemed to take any sting from his words, but she sensed the underlying warning. Feeling like a rabbit retreating cowardly, she tried to concentrate on the countryside they were travelling through. It must be because of the French blood in her veins that she could feel herself responding already to the warmth and wild beauty of the scenery around her. She had told herself emphatically that this could never be her country, yet, after just one day, she was beginning to wonder. Experimentally she turned her face towards the sun and found it pleasant.

'Do you really farm wild bulls and horses, *monsieur*?' she asked eagerly, recalling what her mother had told her.

This time he showed no reluctance to talk, nor did he appear to think it strange that she hadn't mentioned she knew anything of his occupation until now. 'I have two properties, *mademoiselle*. On one I do indeed breed bulls and horses, but the wild white horses run anywhere. They are free, like the wind.'

'And on the other?'

'There the land is richer. There are vines and cornfields, rich orchards. In the Camargue and its neighbourhood, you will always find contrast, *ma chère*, and in everything that's different you will find something to delight you.'

Julia nodded, letting his growing enthusiasm warm

her. In him she sensed a strong love of his native land, but she shivered as she also sensed that his hatred for anyone who did anything to destroy it might be stronger. He would consider she was privileged, in allowing her to come and live here, and heaven help her if she did anything to abuse his hospitality!

'On which of the estates do you live, *monsieur*?' She asked hastily.

'Your aunt and I prefer the wild bulls and the marshes,' he shrugged. 'You may not, but you will soon adapt.'

It appeared she would have to, as it didn't seem she was to be given a choice. 'I'm looking forward to meeting Aunt Mavis,' she said, again managing not to answer his comment directly.

'You will meet your cousin, my half-sister, too,' he told her. 'Fayme is married with children of her own and lives in Nice, but she will be visiting us next week.'

'I knew I had a cousin, but I didn't know she was married.' Julia bit her lip, thinking it was sad that relations could so lose touch with one another.

'Your parents were sent an invitation to the wedding,' Guy Guerard assured her curtly.

Julia sighed. 'I think they travelled so widely that a lot of their mail never caught up with them. Otherwise I'm sure they would have come.'

'No matter,' he shrugged abruptly, as if something which had happened so long ago didn't interest him anymore. 'I'm sure you will enjoy the twins, when they arrive. They are six and proper little devils.'

'Do they stay with you often, *monsieur*?' Julia smiled, for she loved children.

'They do,' he replied, somewhat heavily. 'And I think you should call me Guy. If we aren't really related, there is a relationship of a kind.'

'*Merci*,' she said, conscious of a light glow because this seemed evidence that, despite their inauspicious beginning, he had some liking for her. What he said explained, too, his remarks about having experience in handling children, children she had mistakenly concluded must be his own.

'You speak French?' There was faint surprise in his voice.

'Many people do.'

'I know that,' he retorted impatiently, increasing his speed on a straighter stretch of road. As the powerful car responded swiftly, he added, 'When you made no attempt to, I decided you didn't.'

'I learnt at school and my mother taught me.' Her eyes pleaded forgiveness for her sharpness as he glanced at her and he nodded slightly, as if aware of her remorse.

There was a faint warmth in his face as he broke into rapid French which deepened in approval as she followed him easily and replied in the same language. 'Your accent is good,' he acknowledged. 'It will be useful if I can't find you an English-speaking husband.'

The meekness, which she sensed pleased him, dissolved into anger. 'You can't be serious!' she exclaimed. 'I know you mentioned a husband when we first met, yesterday, but I thought that was only because you were annoyed with me!'

'You thought I was merely teasing?' As their eyes clashed, he observed the sparks in hers coldly before giving his attention to the road again. 'I don't talk idly, Julia. I've already told you I have a great many responsibilities, some which I find extremely irksome and have no wish to add to. A young girl is a great responsibility, make no mistake about that. However, you don't have to marry the first man I present to you who shows interest. I am not inhuman, you know.'

'That might be a matter of opinion, *monsieur*,' she retorted acidly. 'You may approve of your outdated customs, but I consider they belong to the Dark Ages! Did you arrange your sister's marriage too?'

'My sister's marriage need not concern you.' The

continuing coldness of his tones suggested an anger matching her own. 'And before you criticise our customs, you might be wise to study your own. On the whole marriages in France appear to have a greater success rate than yours in the U.K., which must surely prove something!'

Julia sighed. It was a topic over which they might argue for hours and she would rather leave it until she was feeling less tired and her wits were sharper. She was well aware that many marriages in France were still arranged, but she couldn't see herself marrying a man she didn't love.

'I must take after my mother, I'm afraid,' she answered rebelliously.

'If she hadn't run away she might have been alive today, *mademoiselle*.'

Julia flinched, conscious of a hardness in Guy Guerard which she seemed to have the knack of arousing. 'I'm sure neither of us is in a position to judge,' she said stiffly. 'Wouldn't you be tempted to elope if you loved someone and wanted to marry them and your family were all against it?'

'I would never be tempted to give up what I have for any woman,' he retorted curtly.

Biting her lip, Julia held back a sharp retort, realising, as she had done moments ago, that it might be futile to argue. There was something wholly primitive about this man, something untamed and untamable, which disturbed her more than she would have thought possible. He was a wealthy estate owner, in all respects a man of superior intelligence with other interests, yet, at the same time, he made no attempt to conceal that in his blood there still flowed plenty of the plundering, dominating instincts of the ancient Gauls.

Apparently believing he had had the last word, he lapsed into a grim silence, leaving her alone with her thoughts. The silence wasn't a comfortable one and as there was nothing to take her mind off it but huge stretches of salt marshes, she felt relieved beyond measure when they breasted a slight rise and in front of them stood a large rambling mansion surrounded by gardens, trees and low scrub and backed by a range of massive stone buildings.

'Your house, *monsieur*?' she asked, wide-eyed.

'My home,' he corrected.

'It's impressive.' She couldn't think of another word that might describe it more aptly. It wasn't beautiful, as a French chateau might be, the lines were too rugged. It was as uncompromising as the man by her side, but, like him, it wasn't a house one would forget in a hurry. 'How old is it?' she asked, quite unconscious of the awe in her voice.

'Old enough to have a few ghosts, *mademoiselle*,' he allowed.

'Really?' Julia turned a startled face to him, her grey eyes faintly apprehensive.

'No,' he smiled, relenting. 'At least, I haven't seen any, but the original house dates back several centuries and has been in my family for countless generations. I believe we were some of the plundering Saracens.'

'Or perhaps the Moors—or Turks?' she laughed, feeling a faint stirring of something she hated to think could be pride.

'Really, *mademoiselle*!' he cast her a mocking glance. 'If I didn't know otherwise, I might suspect you were familiar with our barbaric past!'

His dark eyes, trained on her, mesmerised her slightly. She put it down to fright when the pulse in her slim white throat began beating rapidly. Rather incoherently she stammered, 'As my mother was French, I suppose some of them might have been my ancestors too.'

'Undoubtedly.' His glance flicked to the road before returning to her consideringly. 'I find it enlightening that you have shown an interest. For me it will be interesting to discover which is stronger, your English or your French blood, Julia.'

When they drove into the courtyard in front of the house, their journey at an end, Julia was relieved. Guy's too astute observations embarrassed her and she felt she wouldn't be sorry to get away from him for a while. She couldn't believe the other members of his family were anything like him.

He left the car as she drew an uncertain hand over dazed eyes. 'Come along, Julia,' he drew her gently from the passenger seat. 'One would imagine you had never seen a house like this before.'

'I haven't,' she confessed, stumbling beside him, causing his grip to tighten on her arm.

'I hope you will enjoy living here,' he said formally, while his expression suggested that if she didn't she would just have to make the best of it.

She glanced at him suspiciously, but before she had time to reply two small boys burst from the house and ran towards them. Julia guessed immediately that they were the twin sons of Guy's half-sister, they looked so much alike. They were young and dark with dancing eyes and curly hair and full of bouncing energy.

'*Bonsoir*, Oncle Guy!' they cried, confirming her suspicions. '*Nous sommes en vacances!*'

As they greeted their uncle and told him they were here on holiday, Julia heard Guy draw a deep breath. 'Since when?' he asked, frowning sternly.

'Lorraine brought us,' they told him, as he bent over them, gently rumpling their hair, 'Maman and Papa had to go away.'

'Not again?' Guy Guerard's mouth tightened ominously, but as he obviously restrained himself a gay voice broke in quickly.

'Don't be cross, Guy, *chéri*. Léon had to go to Germany and begged Fayme to go with him. You know how it is, they are still very much in love, but Fayme didn't agree until I offered to come and look after the boys. We were sure you wouldn't mind.'

Julia, reluctantly lifting her head from her interested

contemplation of the two boys, saw standing beside them a young woman whose appearance proved even more charming than her voice. And she was gazing at Guy Guerard with a very proprietorial expression in her eyes.

CHAPTER TWO

THE girl who had so quietly approached them was tall and dark, in her late twenties and very beautiful. There was a sudden short silence during which Julia felt Guy Guerard stiffen before he appeared to relax.

Releasing his hold of Julia's arm, he took the stranger's proffered hand. '*Bonsoir*, Lorraine,' lifting her hand to his mouth, he kissed it lightly. 'My sister is too fond of leaving her offspring to exhaust others. I must have a word with her.'

'I assure you I don't mind.' Lorraine smiled at him intimately, ignoring Julia.

'We must make sure you don't!'

'*Merci*,' Lorraine laughed, 'but it will be a pleasure! I am very fond of children.'

One of Guy's brows rose slightly as he drew her forward. 'You must meet Fayme's cousin, whom I have just escorted from London. She has come to make her home with us, Lorraine.' Coolly he introduced the two girls, then the twins.

Lorraine merely nodded distantly at Julia before returning her attention to Guy. 'Madame has been telling me about her.'

Julia wished the girl wouldn't talk as though she wasn't there and that her tone wasn't quite as patronising. Guy, however, didn't seem to notice anything wrong. Julia wondered if he was too dazzled by Lorraine's beauty to be aware of her lack of manners? He was smiling at her, his dark eyes wandering flatteringly over her, and Julia spoke quickly to the twins in order not to see how charming he could be when he chose.

The two boys, Fortune and Fitz, were disposed to be

24

friendly, showing an immediate liking for Julia which warmed her heart. They had a habit of speaking in unison which she found intriguing. It was as if they could read each other's thoughts and often thought of the same thing, at the same time.

'Is your hair real, *mademoiselle*?' they asked, gazing at her curiously, 'It's like pale gold silk.'

'That's enough, boys!' Lorraine intervened sharply, as Guy ushered them all inside. Clearly if there were any compliments going she wanted them for herself.

'I'm sure they didn't mean any harm,' Julia retorted quickly, as their small faces fell.

'Julia is tired, boys,' Guy spoke smoothly. 'I feel sure if you go to the kitchen, you will find your supper is ready. It must be more than time for your bath and bed and you will be able to talk to Julia in the morning.'

They obeyed him without demur. For all they were high-spirited youngsters, Julia noticed they immediately recognised their uncle's authority. '*Au revoir*,' they chorused, as they ran off.

Lorraine made no attempt to go with them, to supervise their bedtime, and though Julia was suddenly nervous at the prospect of meeting her aunt, she couldn't help wondering just how seriously Lorraine took her promise to Guy's sister. She seemed more interested in Guy than the twins.

As she hung back uncertainly, Lorraine caught Guy's hand, the twins apparently forgotten as she gazed up at him appealingly. 'When you have taken Miss Ward to meet Madame, could we go somewhere and talk, Guy?'

Guy smiled at her gently. 'It would be a pleasure, *ma chère*, but I'm afraid if there is anything you wish to discuss it must wait until dinner. I would like Julia settled in, then I have much to see to.'

'But of course,' the French girl pouted a little but returned his smile brilliantly. 'You must forgive me, *mon cher*. I haven't seen you for three weeks and it makes me impatient.'

How Guy would have replied, Julia didn't discover,
as a woman entered the massive hall from a door at the
opposite end of it. She was middle-aged with grey hair
and a kindly expression. She walked slowly, Julia
noticed, with a limp, and, as she neared them, her lined
face lit up, then saddened.

'It is Julia, is it not? Why did no one tell me you had
arrived?' she exclaimed, her eyes glazed with tears as
she held out her arms. 'I would have known you
anywhere, *petite*, you are so like your dear mother.'

Later, as Julia was shown to her room by Hortense,
the elderly housekeeper, she tried dazedly to piece
together the trauma of the past hour. She felt so tired
that she couldn't be sure of recalling anything with
strict accuracy, and she wondered why she should be
feeling so curiously discouraged. She refused to believe
it had anything to do with Lorraine Lichine. After Guy
had left them in the salon, after refusing the
refreshments brought by Hortense, Lorraine had stared
at Julia silently, rendering her unable to talk naturally
to Mavis Guerard. She had found Lorraine's fixed,
malicious stare upsetting, particularly as she could
think of no reason for it.

Lorraine was clearly attracted to Guy Guerard, and
if she, as Julia suspected, nurtured hopes of marrying
him, she couldn't possibly believe Julia was a threat to
her chances. Lorraine wouldn't know of Guy's plans to
marry off the little nuisance from England, at the first
opportunity, and certainly not to himself! Julia
wondered if he would tell her.

The staircase was curved and wide, with what seemed
to be a hundred steps, the corridor leading off it even
longer. At last Hortense paused outside a wide, white
door. 'You will sleep here, *mademoiselle*,' she said, with
a kind smile. 'I think you will be very comfortable.
Your cases have already been unpacked and dinner is at
eight-thirty.'

When she had gone, Julia walked into the room,

glancing around eagerly. It was large and comfortable if not wholly feminine. Already she was seeing ways of making it brighter and had to remind herself she was only here for a few weeks. She had a sudden, brilliant flash of inspiration. Perhaps if she mentioned that to Lorraine, the other girl might like her better.

She had only intended sitting on the edge of the bed, she hadn't meant to stretch out on it. Realising what she was doing, she half rose again then lay back with a weary shrug. Did it matter what she did? Aunt Mavis had also gone to her room and she was sure no one else would bother. Carelessly she kicked off her shoes, and, lacing her hands behind her head, gazed abstractedly at the ceiling.

Thinking of the twins brought a smile to her face; she wondered what they were doing. No doubt fast asleep in bed by this time. She could just picture their deceptively angelic little faces, side by side on their pillows. She wished she liked the thought of Lorraine half as much. She was a beautiful young woman, but there was a certain hardness about her. She might make Guy a very suitable wife, but Julia wondered if she would ever make him happy.

Ashamed that her thoughts should cling so tenaciously to matters which were none of her business, Julia closed her eyes, letting the drowsiness which dogged her so persistently these days take over. It was quiet, there wasn't a sound, the evening hush being broken only intermittently by the soft cooing of doves from the trees outside her window. It must have been the doves that lulled her to sleep, she realised afterwards, but she had no idea when it happened.

Some time later she awoke to find someone shaking her gently and twisted in unconscious indignation from the hands arousing her, being quite happy as she was. At last, forcing open drowsy grey eyes, she found herself gazing straight at Guy Guerard.

'This appears to be becoming a habit, *mon enfant*,' he

teased, a glint of humour in the blue eyes staring down on her.

Flushed with embarrassment, Julia struggled to sit up. 'Have I slept long?' she asked anxiously.

Because he was sitting on the edge of the bed with his hands still on her shoulders, it seemed the most natural thing in the world, as she reeled unsteadily, that he should draw her gently to him, until her head rested on his shoulder.

'That I cannot tell, *ma chère*,' she felt his mouth quirk against her forehead. 'When I last saw you, downstairs, you had the heavy-eyed look which I sometimes see in the twins when they are tired, and I guessed what might happen. You were sleeping like an angel, but if I hadn't woken you up, you might never have forgiven me, if you'd missed dinner.'

'I'm not very hungry,' she sighed, but snuggled against him so he would know she wasn't ungrateful. She liked the feel of his arms round her. He wore only a shirt, unbuttoned to his waist, and the dark hair on his chest tickled her cheek while the deep throb of his heart seemed to echo right through her. Innocently she placed her soft palm over it, unconsciously monitoring the heavy beat, but drew a startled breath as a sharp sensation reverberated through her limbs, making her quiver.

'Julia!' With a remonstrating growl he took her hand away although he made no attempt to let her go. 'You are tired and not hungry because you have been ill. Perhaps if I tell you often enough you will believe me, but you must take it easy for a while. Tomorrow you will see a doctor, and Lorraine will make sure the boys don't disturb you until I am able to get in touch with my sister and demand she returns.'

Julia found the hand he had removed, then freed, slipping to the belt of his slacks, and her finger clenched around it in agitation. 'Please,' she pleaded huskily, 'don't send for Fayme on my account. The twins are darlings. I'm sure I shall enjoy helping to look after them.'

'You need looking after yourself, *petite*,' his voice unexpectedly roughened, 'I forbid you to wear yourself out.'

'Well, I certainly don't need a doctor!'

Sighing wryly, he gently massaged her back, as he had done the previous evening. 'You must allow me to be the best judge of that, Julia. It's merely a precaution.'

'So you can get me quickly married off?' Angrily she lifted her head, pulling away from him.

Just as angrily his arms tightened until her face was very near his. Slowly her eyes dropped to his mouth, studying the hard, sensuous lines of it. She had an insane desire to feel the demanding strength of it pressed against her own. Then, suddenly, as she felt the world slipping mysteriously away, tears began running down her cheeks and she heard his muttered exclamation as he saw them.

'I'm sorry, Guy.'

Just as swiftly as she had aroused it, his anger faded and he crushed her face to his shoulder again. 'It will do you good to weep, Julia,' he said softly, running soothing fingers through her hair, brushing them over her temple before curving his hand around her nape. 'The loss of your parents, having no one to turn to, all adds up to shock. Even coming here had to increase your distress before we have had a chance to try and heal it. It is better to let tears wash the misery from your heart so you can gradually learn to be happy again.'

Julia drew a steadying breath. She would never have guessed him to be so understanding, especially after all she had accused him of. Not for a moment did she really believe he meant to marry her off. Somewhere, amidst all the trauma he mentioned, she must have lost her sense of humour. Rubbing her face with the handkerchief he eventually put in her hands, she smiled at him tremulously.

'Thank you,' she whispered, as he bent his head and kissed her very gently.

When Guy kissed her, although she had wanted it herself a few minutes ago, Julia felt immediately stunned. His mouth, at first tender, hardened suddenly as a devastating warmth surged between them. It was strong enough to shatter the ice which had encased her heart for weeks, but she grew wildly frightened. Although he wasn't exerting any real pressure, she had never been kissed like this before and her emotions, which she had always considered very cool, began coming to life too fast for her. Her feelings of panic accelerated as she became increasingly aware of his disturbing masculinity.

She thought she might have to struggle, but in only seconds he was putting her from him. He must be shocked by his own behaviour, Julia decided dazedly, noticing his face was pale, but when he spoke he sounded more amused than anything else.

'When it comes to comforting beautiful young women, a man can get carried away. I should have known better.'

Julia was surprisingly hurt by his laughter, but the pain of his derision did enable her to pull herself together. 'You were merely trying to help, I imagine,' she heard herself replying with commendable coolness. 'You've been very kind.'

'Can you manage to dress?' he asked, his eyes gentle on her flushed cheeks. 'I'm sure Lorraine would be only too happy to assist you.'

'Of course, *mademoiselle*. I am here to be useful,' Lorraine interrupted from the doorway, her voice rather shrill as she walked in on them.

Without meaning to, Julia exclaimed, 'I wish people would knock before entering my room!'

Guy immediately disapproved. 'Lorraine is only

concerned for you, Julia. I can assure you she isn't usually so remiss. As for myself, I did knock, but you were asleep.'

Lorraine shrugged helplessly, increasing Julia's feelings of guilt. 'Madame sent me, she is worried. She wonders if you would prefer to dine in your room this evening. Perhaps something light in your bed, on a tray?'

Julia would have loved to have gone to bed, but was determined to prove she was stronger than she felt.

'I'm grateful,' she said stiffly, 'but I have no intention of making extra work. If I can just have a little privacy, I will be down for dinner in a few minutes.'

Again Guy's mouth tightened, but he obligingly steered Lorraine outside. 'Very well, Julia. If you are sure, we will wait for you in the *salon*.'

Had her ridiculous, if small, show of antagonism been worth seeing, Guy would have placed his arm protectively around Lorraine's waist? Determined not to dwell on it, as soon as the door closed behind them Julia reached in her wardrobe for one of her older dresses. After showering quickly in the adjoining bathroom, she put it on. She still looked washed out and felt anything more glamorous than the slightly faded print would merely serve to emphasise her pallor. Wishing the rest of her would fill out like her breasts, she cast them a disparaging glance. Although her derriere was attractively rounded, her waist was very narrow, and though she didn't mind her legs being long and slender, she knew her shoulders and wrists were too thin.

Flushing a little because of such surprising self-absorption, which, strangely, had only started the evening before, Julia turned sharply from the mirror into which she had been unconsciously staring and began searching for a handkerchief to take with her. If she was becoming prone to tears, she thought wryly, she'd better be prepared. Guy might not be willing to lend his handkerchief indefinitely!

Her lips still tingled from his kiss as she went downstairs, but she warned herself not to make too much of it. As he said, he had only meant to be comforting. She wondered if he was in love with Lorraine. Lorraine mightn't have much shape, but she had a beautiful face and a cool air of sophistication Julia envied. She hadn't missed the inviting glances thrown at Guy by the other girl, but there had been no time to ascertain his true feelings. With his looks, Julia guessed women ran after him, but whether he pursued them as enthusiastically remained to be seen. Julia had no doubt that before long she might find out and, mysteriously, the coldness she thought had gone from her heart returned.

They dined in a room of graceful proportions and some style, the gleaming furniture, the shining silver and satin curtains hinting more clearly than words might have done that the Guerards were not a poor family. Was it surprising that women like Lorraine cast a covetous eye on the owner of so much wealth? Julia thought scornfully.

Playing with her *loup farci Niçois*, a delicious fish dish which her aunt assured her contained all the flavours of Provençe, Julia took little part in the conversation going on around her. It wasn't until Guy spoke to her rather curtly that she looked up with a start.

'Is everything to your liking, Julia?'

Swallowing quickly, she nodded, jolted by the unexpected anger in his face. He was a force to be reckoned with in pale blue silk and dark grey worsted, but it was the coldness of his eyes that struck her most forcibly. Whatever she had done to warrant such grimness she couldn't think, unless it had been her rudeness to Lorraine.

'You aren't eating.'

'We have just began, *monsieur*.'

'You left half your *jus de tomate*.'

The others had had soup, a rich *potage* which she had felt she couldn't face. Now she groped for another excuse. 'If you will give me time, *monsieur*.'

Mavis Guerard, seeming amused yet slightly worried by their exchange, broke in quickly. 'Don't harass the child, Guy! Pour her a little more Sancerre. It may improve her appetite and make her feel better.'

Julia, who had drunk her first glass almost straight off, as it had seemed easier than eating, didn't want any more but wasn't quick enough to prevent him doing as his stepmother requested. Before she could snatch her glass out the way, he had refilled it.

'It's very kind of you,' she protested, 'But I'm not used to it.'

'It pleases your aunt and might put a little colour in your cheeks,' he retorted, apparently losing interest as he turned to Lorraine again.

After dinner they went back to the *salon* for coffee, and later Lorraine put on some dreamy music and danced with Guy. Julia was surprised that Guy danced so easily and that he and his partner didn't seem at all out of place circling slowly at one end of the huge room.

'Sometimes we dance on the terrace.' Mavis noticed Julia watching the others and turned to her. 'Fayme is very fond of dancing, but Guy isn't often as enthusiastic.'

'Does he run the estate himself?' Julia felt guilty about asking, but she was curious.

'Yes,' her aunt nodded, 'He has good men, of course, because he has affairs elsewhere which he must attend to, but mostly he's in charge here. After making sure my daughter and I had enough for our needs, my late husband left him everything, and he has never abused that trust. He has been as a son to me and I hope, one day, he will find a good woman to marry, because I'm sure he will make just as good a husband.'

'Lorraine?' Julia's eyes flew to the other girl, the

question she knew she had no business to ask, hovering on her unsteady lips.

'Perhaps.'

Julia was learning that her aunt either said a lot or very little and she could be discreet. 'I shouldn't have asked,' she murmured unhappily.

Mavis patted her hand. 'Do not let it worry you, dear, there's nothing wrong in showing interest. And even if you were curious, I prefer people with some human failings. Lorraine went to school with Fayme so we have known her many years and she is a frequent visitor. This time she's supposedly here to help look after Fayme's children. More than this I can't tell.'

Julia nodded and tried not to let the sight of Lorraine clasped in Guy's arms disturb her. They stayed at the other end of the room and Guy didn't ask Julia to dance. As she didn't feel up to it, she knew she would have had to refuse if he had, but, she told herself, with a bitterness she didn't understand, it would have been nice to have been asked. She and Mavis chatted idly, mostly about the twins, until her aunt noticed how pale she was growing and sent her to bed.

As Julia rose obediently, Mavis caught one of her hands in both hers. 'Tomorrow, child,' she murmured sadly, 'if the doctor will allow it, we'll speak of your parents. By then we might feel composed enough to talk rationally.'

Julia was determined to be up and about the next day, before the doctor, whom she had no wish to see, arrived. But he came too early. Guy brought him to her room almost before she had time to open her eyes. He did wait outside while the doctor examined her, but as soon as the doctor finished he returned, a very determined expression on his face.

'Well, *comment ça va* Elroy?' he asked grimly.

'Exhaustion,' the doctor replied. He was a tall man who spoke impeccable English and French and, Julia suspected, was no ordinary doctor. He would be a specialist of some kind, at least. She shuddered to think what his fees would be and looked at Guy reproachfully.

He was too busy questioning the doctor to take any notice of her agitation. 'Shouldn't she stay in bed?'

'No, my friend, that won't be necessary. Just see that she gets plenty of rest and fresh air. The loss of her parents, influenza. One without the other would have been enough, but she is young and resilient and should soon recover.'

After escorting the doctor out, Guy returned. Because the doctor hadn't pronounced her beyond hope, having come to much the same verdict as Guy had himself, she hadn't expected to see him again so soon. She was busy getting out of bed when he came back and, alarmed, she did a kind of nose-dive under the sheets. When she emerged, she was annoyed to find him laughing at her.

'I have seen you with as little on before, *ma chérie*. Such modesty becomes you, but there is no need for it with me.'

Glancing at his tall, hard-packed figure, the dark, passionate lines of his mouth, she wasn't so sure. 'I like to think it is habit, *monsieur*,' she answered primly.

'Why do you so frequently resort to that?' he seated himself on the edge of the bed. 'The name's Guy.'

'It—it's because you annoy me at times.' She could have added that it might sometimes be an unconscious attempt to remind herself of the distance between them. 'You make me forget how kind you've been.'

'As long as you remember occasionally,' he accepted her rather muddled apology dryly before proceeding to lay down the law as to what she mustn't do. The things she could do made a tedious list too. She was to have breakfast in bed, coffee on the terrace in the sun; a walk before lunch with a rest afterwards.

'Stop!' she protested, before he was halfway through, 'I'll never remember it all!'

'You'd better,' he threatened, 'or, *mon Dieu*, I will personally see to it that my orders are carried out!'

'Bully!' she cried, incensed by the hardness of his voice.

'And more!' he promised curtly. 'You may regret never having a father near enough to spoil you, but you were also in need of him to smack a little obedience into you. That delightful posterior of yours, Julia, might never have known a man's hand, but it soon could do!'

As a gasp of anger jerked her upright, her thin nightgown strained over curves suddenly tautened by a deeply drawn breath, his eyes fastened on her with speculative humour. 'Temper brings a flattering colour to your cheeks, Julia. I can quite well see that once it is there permanently, along with your other enticing attributes, I might have little difficulty in finding you a good husband.'

With that he got up and walked out of the room.

Julia was so furious that she had no intention of obeying Guy, but each time she decided not to, she remembered his threats and her courage failed her. During the next few days she found herself following his dictates almost to the letter, and, although she despised herself for being so subservient, when the doctor announced himself delighted with her progress she had to admit Guy might have been right. She was both looking and feeling better, and if she hadn't yet put on much weight she no longer looked as though a puff of wind might blow her away.

At first she had been content to talk to her aunt or wander in the gardens with the twins, who, having obviously been forbidden to engage her in any of their unruly games, followed her around like small shadows. She saw little of Lorraine, who always appeared to be off with Guy somewhere. Sometimes she wondered wryly if Lorraine, in agreeing to come here, had imagined she could be in two places at once. It was true that before she pursued Guy to some far corner of the estate, she usually saw to it that one of the maids was around to help look after the twins, but Julia knew that if she had been left more or less in charge of them she couldn't have neglected them so easily.

For all Guy paid Lorraine a lot of attention and seemed to find her attractive, Julia still couldn't decide if he was in love with her or not. She tried not to let herself dwell on it, and there was plenty to occupy her thoughts elsewhere. Aunt Mavis liked her company and the twins were with her constantly, and eventually, as both her strength and courage grew stronger, she ventured farther afield and got to know some of the *gardiens* who worked on the estate.

The French *gardien* is the counterpart of the American cowboy, the bull graziers who look after the herds of cattle and horses in the Camargue. Julia found them a very likeable lot and she hoped they liked her too. From them she learnt much about the immediate locality, and they always seemed to have time to explain to her anything she wanted to know. She enjoyed talking to them although she often found their French somewhat difficult to follow. When she asked Guy about this, he smiled and said that in this respect France was like almost any other country, some districts had almost a language of their own.

He approached her in the garden, one warm morning, when she was surprisingly alone, but she was happy to see him. She was wearing a cotton sundress in a soft yellow which her parents had bought her the last time she had been abroad with them and the colour was flattering to her. She was aware of Guy's eyes on her, and as always when she found him looking at her intently a faint colour stole under her fine skin.

'You are recovering rapidly, Julia.'

'Yes,' she turned to him eagerly as he sat down on the bench beside her, 'I'm feeling much better.'

'Your heart is healing a little, too, I hope?'

'Yes.' She had been aware for a while that it no

longer actually hurt to think of her father and mother, but that Guy had cared enough to ask moved her strangely. To hide an emotion which seemed threatening to overwhelm her, she asked rather abruptly about the *gardiens*.

After he had explained that many Provençals spoke a kind of French she might find difficult to understand, he said dryly, 'You must be feeling better if you have taken the trouble to get to know my men.'

Sensing a kind of underlying criticism, she nearly said that at least she didn't spend as much time with them as he did with Lorraine, but she knew this would be unreasonable. He and Lorraine were old friends while she was a stranger, and he might feel obliged to warn her not to get too familiar with strange men.

'Fortune and Fitz introduced me to some of them when they were showing me around the buildings one day,' she told him quietly, as always wanting to hold on to any harmony between them. 'I don't think it was something I could have managed by myself.'

His mouth thinned. 'I trust the twins are behaving themselves? I have told them not to follow you around.'

'But they aren't any trouble!' she exclaimed indignantly. 'I hope you didn't tell them I was complaining! After all, they've only got me.'

Guy smiled, although he didn't look so amused. 'It isn't Mavis's fault that she can't do more, not in her state of health.'

Julia said mutinously, lowering her thick lashes, 'Lorraine is the one who's supposed to be looking after them. I heard her say myself it was the reason she was here.'

Julia wished she had never said that when she heard the reproval in Guy's voice. 'She never leaves them unless one of the maids is with them, and I would rather you didn't criticise my guests.'

'I'm sorry,' she whispered, unable to look at him,

partly because his defence of Lorraine made her heart grow cold.

'Never mind,' he sighed deeply, with a slight impatience. Then, when she didn't speak, he leaned towards her, raising her bent head by means of his forefinger under her chin, 'You aren't crying, Julia?'

Realising despairingly that there were tears in her eyes, she tried hurriedly to blink them away.

'Why?' he asked softly.

Helplessly, Julia shook her head. To confess that each time he spoke sharply she felt hurt might betray the odd state of her feelings, yet anything else might sound like an excuse.

'I don't know,' she whispered, not altogether untruthfully.

'Come here.' Gently he pulled her closer until she was completely within the circle of his arms. 'I'm a brute, Julia. Your strength is returning, but you are still vulnerable. I must try and remember.'

Because his arms were, as always, so comforting, she made no attempt to escape. He had held her like this before, and she hadn't forgotten how his chest was so broad that when she snuggled into it she felt like a ship safe in port during a storm. It was quiet in the garden, she could have stayed there all day.

As if he was reluctant to let her go, Guy began smoothing the hair from her hot young face. 'Your hair is beautiful, Julia,' he said rather tautly. 'Since you began getting better it has a lovely sheen.'

'You'll turn my head, Guy.' Her tears immediately disappearing, she smiled up at him.

'Is it possible?' he grinned, as if striving for a lighter note, but he suddenly bent over her as if he couldn't help it. She saw his mouth coming nearer and made no attempt to avoid it.

His lips touched hers gently, but, as before, the gentleness instantly changed as the now familiar sensation of heat leapt between them. Julia gulped, more than a little frightened by the feelings he was arousing. He was taking his time. It was almost as if he had forgotten where he was and what he was doing. She could feel the exploring movements of his mouth, moving caressingly along the edge of her bottom lip and suddenly her body felt on fire. She found herself straining against him, her grey eyes turning to purple as she began feverishly returning his kisses.

Immediately she began responding, he raised his head, a coolness entering his eyes as he started moving away. Releasing her clinging arms from around his neck, he jumped to his feet. 'I must go, Julia. I forgot, I have an appointment.'

'Guy?' she whispered, her eyes still dark from aroused feelings.

The swing of his tall body as he turned from her, seemed to emphasise his maleness. He was dressed casually in a light shirt that stretched across the breadth of his shoulders while dark blue slacks fitted tightly over muscular thighs. He was altogether too impressive, she thought weakly, too handsome for any girl's peace of mind. She tried to say something to keep him with her, but her voice would only make a strangled sound in her throat.

If he heard, he took no notice. He merely lifted his hand in a gesture of farewell as he strode towards the house.

Julia sat where she was in a kind of daze after he had gone, trying to fight the still surging force of her own emotions. She was just rubbing a hand over her forehead with a puzzled sigh when Lorraine arrived. Unlike Guy, Lorraine didn't sit down but remained standing.

'Was that Guy I saw leaving?' she asked coldly.

She must know it was. Julia bit her lip and nodded.

The other girl's eyes glittered with dislike as she took in Julia's disturbed appearance. 'Are you feeling unwell again? You look terribly flushed.'

'The sun's hot . . .' Julia stammered.

Lorraine frowned on her for a moment, then said sharply, 'You will find that the sun isn't the only thing that is hot in France, Miss Ward. Perhaps I should warn you.'

Julia was trying to decide what Lorraine meant when she went on. 'Men's passions here can be just as searing. A few Englishmen, I'll admit, have warmer blood in their veins, but few can compare with that of a Frenchman.'

'I still don't see what you're getting at.' Julia stirred uncomfortably under Lorraine's vindictive stare, wondering how much she had seen.

Lorraine gave one of her expressive shrugs. 'I wouldn't have thought you were dimwitted as well as naïve, Julia. What I am trying to tell you, for your own good, is that while Guy might find your innocence a temptation, he would never take you seriously. He might amuse himself with you, but he would never marry you. If anyone is going to be his wife, Julia, it is going to be me!'

CHAPTER THREE

As Julia stared, feeling extremely embarrassed and at a loss for words, Lorraine swung around, as Guy had done, and left her.

'Wait—please wait!' as Lorraine walked away, Julia attempted to stop her, but with a disdainful toss of her head, Lorraine ignored her. Julia had been going to tell her that she wasn't interested in Guy, at least not in the same way as Lorraine was, and that she didn't intend staying here much longer. Half rising from where she was sitting, believing she ought to run after Lorraine and tell her so, Julia sank back with a resigned sigh. If Lorraine wasn't willing to even give her a hearing, then why should she bother?

Julia stayed on in the garden, in the shade of the willow trees, but the peaceful atmosphere had been shattered. Whereas before, her mind like her body had been in a state of lazy somnolence, now she found it impossible to relax. She couldn't help wondering why Lorraine should think she was a threat to her marriage plans. Lorraine might have seen Guy kissing her, but surely she didn't suppose she was the first girl he had kissed, or that it had meant anything. In Julia's case it had merely been a chaste salute which had got slightly out of hand. Nothing for Lorraine to worry about.

Julia sighed again, but this time it was a more tremulous sound. Why was it that whenever she and Guy got too near each other something seemed to happen which drew them even closer? It was as if both their emotions and their bodies became magnetised, one to the other. Yet even this, she realised, might be gross exaggeration. She could be widely off the mark. Probably when Guy kissed a girl, it was often just to amuse himself, not because he felt moved by any deeper feelings.

Slowly Julia wandered back to the house, so lost in thought as to be scarcely aware of where she was going. When the twins came racing around the corner, in search of her, nearly knocking her over, she was almost glad of the diversion they created. As they pretended she was hurt and had to be fussed over and hugged better, she joined laughingly in their game of makebelieve, relieved that something could make her forget their uncle for a few minutes.

'Lunch is ready,' they told her, when they recovered their breath. 'Hortense sent us to find you,' they added importantly.

'Then we mustn't keep her waiting, must we?' Julia smiled, looking down on their happy little faces as they led her back the way they had come.

The first Julia heard of the forthcoming dinner party was when Mavis happened to mention idly that Guy was giving one, the following evening. This was a week after the incident in the gardens, and Julia felt rather hurt that she had heard nothing about it until now.

'Why?' she asked bluntly, somehow not caring if she sounded ill-mannered. 'Is it because of something special?'

'No.' Mavis looked slightly puzzled by Julia's unusual truculence. 'Perhaps I should have told you sooner, but Guy only decided a few days ago. He thinks you should begin meeting some of our neighbours. Getting to know some younger people. You've been here almost a month and it's nearly two since your parents died.'

'I see,' Julia murmured, not seeing at all, or reluctant to.

'I love having you here,' Mavis went on happily. 'It's like having Fayme at home again, and we feel we must do our best for you.'

This seemed too good a chance for Julia to miss, to

give her aunt a little hint about the future. 'You've been more than kind,' she said warmly, 'and I'll always remember and be grateful, but I will have to think of finding something to do. I can't stay with you indefinitely.'

'But why not?' Mavis looked bewildered. 'I thought you understood you were to make your home with us? You surely don't want to return to England, do you?'

'No, not really,' Julia admitted honestly. 'Guy did invite me to live here, but I can't believe he meant me to take him seriously. Anyway, I can't just sit round idly for the rest of my life. It wouldn't be good for me.'

'But you don't sit around idly!' Mavis declared earnestly. 'You do quite a lot. You help me, particularly on days when I find it difficult to get about, and, although perhaps I shouldn't say it, I don't know how I should have managed the twins but for you.'

She didn't mention Lorraine, and, as the other girl had long since given up any pretence of looking after the boys, neither did Julia. 'Their mother will be back soon,' she pointed out practically, 'and if I wasn't here you have plenty of staff.'

Mavis clearly felt hurt. 'Ah, but that's not the same thing, Julia. Our maids are good, but they could never be the same as one's own flesh and blood. No, put all this nonsense about leaving out of your head. When you marry will be soon enough!'

Unfortunately Guy chose that very moment to come upon them, and to Julia's dismay, Mavis began reciting everything she had said. Not only did she get quite excited, she also managed to look extremely upset as she begged him to try and persuade Julia to stay.

Guy said little, but his face was hard with disapproval as he calmed Mavis down then dragged Julia off to his office. 'You appear to have a genius for upsetting people,' he snapped. 'You do it constantly with Lorraine.'

This was so untrue as to render Julia speechless as he

thrust her inside the small, compact room and slammed the door. 'For two pins,' he continued, 'I would slap you senseless, if only for the pleasure of relieving my feelings!'

'I'm sorry,' she murmured, hoping this might appease him, even if she felt she had nothing to apologise for. She was shaking a little, she couldn't seem to help it, and because he still had hold of her, she was sure he must feel it.

He did, and his teeth came together with a snap which made her even more nervous as she feared he meant to carry out his former threats. Then to her relief, he relented, if with a rather weary sigh.

'What's the matter with you, Julia?' he asked impatiently. 'We are all trying to do our best for you but perhaps you feel we aren't doing enough.'

'You know you are,' she whispered unhappily.

'Then what's wrong?' he persisted.

Julia, reluctant to repeat again everything she had tried to explain to her aunt, even if she had been sure of a more sympathetic audience, merely shook her head.

Studying her keenly, he appeared to be turning things over in his mind. 'Your health seems to be improving daily and you're out a lot with the twins. My *gardiens* are even teaching you to ride. Taking everything into account, I could have sworn you were beginning to enjoy yourself.'

Her eyes widened. She hadn't thought he took any notice of what she was doing. 'How did you discover I was learning to ride?'

'I make it my business to know what goes on on my own property,' he replied enigmatically.

Julia blushed, feeling quite naïve. Of course he would, he was that kind of man. 'I should have told you,' she murmured anxiously, 'I hope you won't be mad with the *gardiens*. I was watching the horses with the twins, one day, and when I said I couldn't ride the men offered to teach me. They probably weren't serious, but I didn't give them a chance to change their minds.'

'Do you not think they checked with me first?' Guy enquired mildly.

Wryly Julia shrugged. 'I should have guessed!'

Guy smiled, his teeth white against the hard tanned skin of his face. 'Don't worry, *ma petite*, I am quite happy for you to be with them—occasionally. They wouldn't do anything to harm you. Indeed they are always singing your praises. You appear to have charmed them.'

'Then you don't mind?' she asked eagerly, for she enjoyed her riding lessons and would hate to have to give them up.

'Not for the moment,' he allowed, then, more soberly, 'So, as you are apparently settling down happily, what brought on all this talk of leaving, which has upset your aunt?'

Julia wished he hadn't asked as there seemed no way she could avoid answering. 'She said you were giving a dinner party tomorrow and I—well, I gathered it was chiefly for my benefit.'

'It is.'

Why need he be so uncompromising? His tone did nothing to encourage a girl suffering from nervousness. Julia swallowed apprehensively under the cool surveillance of a pair of dark blue eyes and had to force herself to go on. 'I only remarked that I didn't want you spending money introducing me to people I might never meet again. At least,' she hesitated uncertainly, 'I mightn't actually have said those exact words, but that was what I meant, and—well, one thing led to another.'

Guy apparently chose to skip most of her obviously muddled explanation. 'You will see these people again.'

'Not if I go back to England.'

'You can forget that,' he said grimly. 'Wherever you go, you aren't going back there, and I won't have Mavis upset unnecessarily.'

Unhappily Julia nodded. Guy looked so stern it might be folly to argue. He had the knack of taking control, of refusing to be disobeyed. If she were patient he might eventually be willing to discuss the possibilities of a career but instinct warned her she would gain nothing by hurrying him.

'It is time you met some younger people,' she heard him saying coldly, 'and a dinner party is one of the easiest ways of doing it.'

What did he mean—younger people? 'I'm quite content,' to her amazement she almost said—with you, and just stopped herself in time. Hastily she added, '—as I am,' before he could begin to wonder at the rather startled expression in her eyes.

He said, his voice emotionless, 'You wouldn't be for long.'

'How do you know?' she asked fiercely, viewing despairingly the implacable lines of his face. 'I've never been interested in boys my own age.'

'Did I mention boys particularly?' he asked mockingly, making her flush.

'No.' She bent her fair head to hide her hot face. 'No, you didn't, but I can't forget how you once talked of getting me married off.'

'If you didn't remind me so often, I might forget,' Guy said softly.

When he spoke gently, like that, she felt a mass of conflicting emotions. His nearness woke feelings in her she neither liked or understood. She had a fearful conviction that if he did introduce her to some younger men, she would compare them with him and find them terribly lacking.

'I'll go and find Aunt Mavis,' she said quickly, 'and apologise for my thoughtlessness.'

'You can do that later.' He caught hold of her arm again, as if he guessed she was trying to escape him. 'Have you a pair of jeans?' he asked abruptly.

'Yes—Why?' she tried to control the familiar rising

uncertainty his touch always evoked and felt a shiver of fire run through her as his fingers tightened. 'I have one pair.'

'Just one pair?' his mouth quirked. 'You surprise me, Julia. I thought jeans were the modern girl's uniform?'

'I like them,' she confessed, 'but remember we travelled by air and I couldn't bring much with me.'

A wry glimmer lit his eyes. 'I threw a lot of your stuff in a box and asked your landlady to give it to charity—after promising to replace it. You should have reminded me.'

So he could buy her some more? 'It's been so lovely and warm,' she assured him. 'I haven't missed them.'

'You look very sweet in your cotton dresses,' he smiled sardonically, 'but I think it is time I showed you something of the surrounding countryside and roads off the beaten track can be dusty. Go and put on your one pair of jeans, Julia, and meet me outside in five minutes.'

Julia knew her eyes must be shining and she saw no reason to hide the thrill of anticipation which rushed to every part of her. 'Do you really mean it?' she begged breathlessly.

'Yes.' Releasing her, he gave her a firm little push. 'Now, hurry!'

She was at the door, almost stumbling in eager haste, when her face suddenly fell and she turned unwillingly. 'What about Lorraine? Have you forgotten? Shall I go and tell her?'

'Tell her what, *mon enfant*?' he asked absently.

Julia drew a trembling breath as his eyes went closely over her, as she was inadvertently silhouetted against the light streaming through the doorway. 'That we're going out,' she said reluctantly. 'Won't she want to come?'

'No, don't bother,' he replied curtly. 'Someone has to see to the twins.'

Julia had no idea where he intended taking her, but

somehow she didn't care. She felt so happy, just being with him in the big truck, that she couldn't think of anything else. After the misery of her parents' death, when she didn't think she would ever be happy again, she was almost ashamed to realise she was beginning to forget. It was happening slowly and regret would always linger in a part of her, but the actual pain was fading, allowing her to think of other things.

She thought now of Guy's driving. Other men might drive as well, but not many, she suspected, gave their passengers such feelings of confidence as he did.

'You remind me of a London taxi driver,' she said impulsively.

'*Merci!*' he smiled.

'You—you aren't offended?'

'If anything, I'm flattered,' he assured her. 'London taxi drivers are among the best in the world.'

'Yes.' She lapsed into silence, thinking there were many sides to this man sitting beside her. She envied Lorraine if he was going to marry her. Colour stole to her cheeks as she became aware of the trend of her thoughts and she hastened to assure herself she was only thinking of husbands generally. And it wouldn't do to put Guy on a pedestal. His softer moods rarely lasted and he could be pretty dictatorial when he felt like it.

Yet she was unable to prevent herself from staring at him, despite the sensible turn of her thoughts. This afternoon, dressed as he was in tight doe-skin trousers and a shirt which was open at the neck and stretched smoothly across his broad shoulders, he had a heart-stopping air of vitality which Julia vaguely realised contained some degree of very masculine sensuality. She had noticed it before, but only slowly had come to recognise it for what it was. Usually a hint of arrogance, of steely pride in his face hid it, but there must be times, she imagined, with an odd little quiver, when he allowed this side of his nature full rein.

As his eyes turned to meet her unconsciously darkening ones, his mouth quirked with a touch of amusement. 'Now what are you thinking of? Are you still cross with me for ticking you off?'

Julia's colour rose, but she didn't try and pretend she hadn't been caught out. 'No,' she confessed, 'I was just being curious.'

'About me? Now you've made me curious. Am I permitted to ask why?'

'It was nothing.' She felt terribly embarrassed.

'Nothing?'

'I was just wondering why you've never married, and it's none of my business, of course.'

That didn't seem to bother him. 'Perhaps I have been waiting for the right girl.'

'And you've found her?'

This time his expression was more wary. 'I think so, but I'm not sure that she's right for me—or vice versa.'

He must be referring to Lorraine. For some reason he must have doubts. That must be why no engagement had been announced. 'If you'll forgive me for saying so,' she frowned, 'you sound a bit cold-blooded. You know, as if you were considering a business deal when every detail had to be just right. I thought one was either in love or not.'

His mouth tightened. 'Nothing's ever as simple as that, Julia. I'm finding this rather unlooked-for contingency in my personal life far more difficult to contend with than any business deal.'

'Well, if I were you, I would ask her.' Julia wondered at the heaviness of her voice. 'You—you could be pleasantly surprised.'

'I think she would be the one to be surprised,' he said tightly, 'and I don't think pleasantly. I'm not even sure myself yet.'

'I see.' She had been about to be very indiscreet and say that she was almost certain that if he asked Lorraine to marry him she would accept, but that he wasn't apparently sure of his own feelings changed everything. Julia forced herself to look away from him, out of the window and was bewildered to find her spirits rising dramatically. It must be the scenery, she thought, yet she could find nothing in the rather lonely landscape to justify such a change.

Skirting a large stretch of water, Guy pointed out some purple heron and flamingo, alongside various wading birds, but he didn't stop until he reached a wide, tree-screened rise, where, he said, if they were patient a herd of white horses might pass. The wild horses frequently moved to fresh pastures and they might be lucky.

Julia found the short respite in the shade of the tamarisks very welcome in the heat of the afternoon, and, as the noise of their engine died away, several small animals began appearing from the undergrowth. She watched with interest some rabbits until they disappeared in alarm from the path of a hungry fox, but it wasn't until a wild boar snorted by, with an assortment of other wild pigs, that she grew really excited.

'Oh, look!' she grabbed Guy's arm below his rolled up sleeve. 'They look fierce. Are they safe?'

'Probably safer than you might be, if you continue hanging on to me,' he retorted.

Heat rushed to Julia's cheeks and she removed her hand as if she'd been stung. 'I'm sorry,' she choked with embarrassment, 'I meant, are they dangerous?' Then, as she noticed with dismay the marks of her fingers on his skin, she reached out involuntarily to try and rub them away.

'Will you stop doing that!' he said tightly, yet his glance seemed fixed on her slender body, all too clearly revealed against the open neckline of her silky shirt.

Because he sounded so grim, she produced another apology, with what sounded suspiciously like a sob. Hearing it, he cupped her chin, with a low exclamation of remorse, turning it so she was unable to avoid the brooding darkness of his face. She was acutely conscious of the clean, masculine smell of him as his arms went 'round her. 'I'm a brute,' he muttered. 'Come here.'

The front of the truck was roomy, but there were gears and other things between them. There must have been every opportunity to avoid what happened next, yet Julia knew she was helpless to prevent it. She did try to escape but it was a futile gesture. She watched his face coming closer until suddenly everything went out of focus and there was nothing but an increasing feeling of expectancy as his mouth closed softly over her own.

Of their own volition her hands fluttered up to touch his face and hair before creeping round his neck, and then she was holding him tighter and tighter while he was pressing her back against the seat with the weight of his urgent body. His hard mouth crushed her lips apart as his hands found her firm young breasts and his kisses became more demanding as sparks seemed to flare between them, threatening to explode into a consuming fire.

She felt the back of her seat collapse as his hand struck a lever and faint alarm bells began sounding as she lay flat and he began undoing buttons, all the time murmuring words which barely penetrated the curious sense of detachment that flooded her as she waited for the flames surrounding them to swallow her up. She might have been on drugs, there was no resistance in her body, only the sound of her fast-beating pulses and his heart pounding in her ears. Guy's kisses were possessive seduction, weakening her limbs so she could only cling to him as his teeth closed gently on her lower lip and his free hand feathered across her stomach to grip her slim waist.

Somewhere near a horse neighed, followed by the high-pitched scream of a stallion. Julia began shaking uncontrollably and, as Guy stiffened, she gave a muffled cry.

As he heard her, he withdrew, his eyes burning with an intensity which took her breath away. Yet it was quickly cloaked and as he straightened, his face wore its usual aloof expression. His ability to regain command of himself so swiftly made her almost gasp in astonishment.

'Come on, Julia.' Ruthlessly he jerked her upright while his harsh voice did much to restore her to normality. 'If you want to see the horses,' he said coolly. 'You have only a few minutes.'

'The wild horses?' she repeated stupidly.

'Yes.' He turned briefly away so she could do up her shirt.

Her fingers fumbled, but she managed. Beyond the truck strange whitish-grey creatures galloped past, their long manes and tails streaming behind them as they ran. Julia seemed to see them through blurred eyes so that they merged in a pounding, moving mass. She got the impression of barred teeth and savagery and of glorious, unrestricted freedom.

Guy appeared unperturbed and as aloof as before. He was obviously totally unmoved by the experience they had just shared. His eyes returned to study the confusion in her face with a cynical detachment she found difficult to believe.

'Well, what do you think of them?' he asked.

'I'm not sure,' she answered uncertainly. 'I didn't have time to see them properly.'

'Many people have less.'

She felt he was mocking her, and the colour which had left her cheeks returned brightly. 'Why did you kiss me?' she whispered.

He smiled indifferently. 'Surely for some things there doesn't always have to be a reason? In this case, for instance, don't you think a reason might sound too much like an excuse? Blame the circumstances, if you must. The isolation and heat of the day, or merely impulse.'

'Impulse?'

His smile became even more cynical. 'You're a lovely girl, Julia. Perhaps I was caught unawares and you tempted me.'

'You've too much control.'

'Yes. Yet,' his eyes grew shades colder, 'I don't believe anyone is infallible. At least I don't now. Maybe unconsciously, when I held you and kissed you, I was trying to deal with the restraint which you often wear like an armour. If you're to meet other young people, especially young men, I wouldn't wish them to think you weren't capable of being normally friendly. What happened to fill you with so many inhibitions, Julia?'

'You're imagining things,' she protested.

'No, I'm not,' he replied shortly. 'Even Mavis has noticed a certain wariness, and she blames your mother.'

Julia was immediately on the defensive. 'She only told me what men were like!'

'And not to let them near you?'

Did he have to sound so full of grim mockery? 'Is it so odd that a mother should try and protect her own daughter?'

'Didn't she realise the harm she might be doing?' he countered curtly.

'Was that what you were trying to discover when you kissed me?' she cried angrily. 'You kissed me merely as a kind of experiment?'

'In a way,' he admitted impatiently.

His enigmatic confession hurt, but she didn't pause to wonder why as she exclaimed furiously, 'Well, I can do without having you trying to soften me up!'

'It wasn't like that at all,' he retorted tersely, 'although I have satisfied myself on one or two points. Namely,' he grated, as Julia's brows rose in contemptuous enquiry over stormy grey eyes, 'that you're quite capable of all the normal responses. Ironically I've found you're more dangerous than irretrievably damaged.'

A flicker of bewilderment joined the lingering rebellion in Julia's eyes. 'You French have a habit of exaggerating everything, *monsieur*!'

This time it was Guy's brows that rose. 'If you examined your last sentence for a moment, my little half-French cousin, you might find we aren't the only ones.'

Julia sighed, realising he was right, both about that and other things. Biting her lip, she could still hear her mother warning her against the treachery of men. Yet, although Guy was very much a man, she was sure he wasn't like this. If he had designs on a woman and wished to make love to her, Julia felt certain that while he might try persuasion, he would never seduce her against her will.

As he remained silent, she wondered if he was waiting for an apology, but this she refused to give. 'Like I said,' she repeated instead, 'I believe my mother was only trying to protect me.'

'She would have done that better by giving you a settled home,' he retorted.

'She hoped to do so one day,' Julia assured him gravely.

Guy sighed, his mouth a grim line as he edged the truck from under its concealing canopy of trees and drove off. 'I think we've argued enough and it's getting too late to go further. Let's go home.'

Julia's trip out had proved more yet less than she had expected, but she offered no complaint. Guy had shown her little more of the district than she had seen already, but he had been so grimly silent on the way back that she hadn't dared to ask if he would take her out again another day. Lorraine had been waiting for them when they reached the house, and broke into a torrent of angry French which Julia had found impossible to follow. From the one or two words she did manage to

understand, she gathered that Lorraine was furious
with Guy for going off and leaving her. Guy let her
ramble on for a few minutes before ordering her curtly
to shut up, after which Julia discreetly retreated, having
no wish to interfere in what was obviously turning into
a lovers' quarrel!

The next night, the night of the dinner party, she
dressed with care. She wore a black dress, one which
her mother had once bought for herself and discarded.
She had left it behind the last time she had been in
London, and Julia had kept it chiefly because it was
almost all she had to remember her mother by, but also
because it had been so expensive it seemed a shame to
throw it out. Christine Ward, still in her forties, had
been a slender woman, and the dress, though a little
slack, fitted Julia almost perfectly. Yet, as she zipped it
up, she couldn't help feeling doubtful. The low neckline
and narrow, slitted skirt might look right on an older,
more sophisticated woman, but it did nothing for Julia.
Somehow, although it had cost the earth, it managed on
her to look cheap and vulgar.

Still, she told herself stubbornly, wasn't that the effect
she wanted? She refused to make herself beautiful so she
could be paraded before numerous young men, knowing
how much Guy was hoping one of them would take her
off his hands! She had frizzed her hair, having borrowed
Hortense's crimping tongs, and with a heavy make-up,
including loads of eyeshadow and scarlet lip-gloss,
begged from one of the maids, she considered her debut
might be devastating! If the young men had their mothers
with them, and she'd gathered from Guy they would have,
she doubted if they would lose much time in whisking
their endangered sons out of sight of such an obvious siren!

Gazing at her gaudy reflection with renewed
satisfaction, Julia didn't allow herself an opportunity to
feel ashamed as she sprayed herself heavily with a sultry
perfume bought in the nearest village that very
afternoon, and prepared to go downstairs.

She hadn't seen Guy all day. She had missed him at breakfast and he had been out for lunch. Usually she was around when he returned of an evening, but today she had done her best to avoid him, and hoped to avoid him now, until she reached the sanctuary of the *salon*. Once there she could withstand any disapproving glances he might throw at her, but she didn't intend giving him the chance of annihilating her verbally beforehand!

Just when everything appeared to be going well, she never guessed that fate would deal her such a contrary blow! As she opened her bedroom door, to her dismay Guy was in the act of raising a hand to knock on it.

For a moment he paused, his hand frozen in mid-air, as if held there by the force of his icy anger. The look in his eyes struck a chilling note in her heart as they slid over her, doing a swift but thorough inventory. She heard his breath rasp as he exclaimed curtly, 'You aren't going down there in that!'

Julia thought, in brief panic, of the fine shawl in her drawer which, with hindsight, might easily have covered her bare shoulders. But it was too late so she decided to brazen it out. 'I'm just on my way,' she smiled sweetly, hoping that by ignoring his oblique reference to her dress, he would take the hint and not argue over it.

He didn't seem inclined to argue. He appeared to assume she had inadvertently made a mistake which could easily be rectified. 'That dress, wherever you got it, Julia, isn't suitable. You have others?'

'What if I have?' She made the mistake of backing defiantly from the confusing glitter in his eyes, and unfortunately, he followed her into her room, closing the door behind him. 'This is a very nice black dress,' she blustered. 'Everyone in France wears black.'

'For heaven's sake stop generalising about us!' Guy snapped. 'Not everyone in France, especially *jeune filles*, wears black. And,' his mouth tightened, 'what have you done with your hair? It resembles a bush!'

'Just—well, I've curled it a little . . .'

'A little? *Mon Dieu*, You look like a tart!'

She flushed crimson. 'How—how dare you!'

'And your perfume—ugh!' his face hardened in disgust as his nostrils twitched. 'Instead of presenting you to my friends as a suitable daughter-in-law, I should be sending you to the Folies-Begère. In a very short time I have no doubt you would be the toast of Paris!'

It was altogether too much! Now he had come out in the open, despite his fine pretences, he did mean to try and marry her off! Julia was glad she had dressed like this, and like this she was determined to remain!

'What did you want, *monsieur*?' she asked coldly, deciding, after all his insults, she could never call him Guy again.

Without taking his grim eyes off her, he held up a small case she hadn't noticed him carrying. 'I brought you a necklace. Mavis and I thought you might like to wear it.'

'I already have one.'

'A diamond one?' Guy flicked open the case and the beautiful simplicity of the stones shone out at them.

Julia caught her breath. 'No,' she confessed, 'I've never had anything as valuable, but I'm afraid it wouldn't go with my dress.'

'I agree,' his eyes glinted ominously, like two cold chips of blue steel. 'This piece of jewellery was meant to be worn by a *jeune fille*, not what you appear to have turned yourself into, in the past hour!'

'Well, I don't want it!' she retorted, not very politely.

'As I've told you before,' he said savagely, 'You've had altogether too much of your own way.' With a harsh note in his voice, he advanced. 'Are you going to obey me? Do you intend being reasonable and removing that dress and make-up? I'll give you one more chance to change your mind, but I must remind you that we are expecting guests and haven't got much time.'

Julia swallowed convulsively, trying to hang on to any courage she could find. Guy Guerard was over six foot and his shoulders were broad. When he was angry, his eyes smouldering, his face an iron mask, he was a terrifying sight. He hadn't yet put on his dinner jacket, but even in his shirt and dark pants he was a force to be reckoned with. He reminded her somehow of the dangerous wild stallion that had thundered past them the previous day.

'Well?' he prompted grimly.

'No!' Haughtily she shook her head, knowing she was shaking, despite her obvious bravado, but bent on defying him.

'That is your last word?'

'Yes.' What else would her pride allow her to say? And, although he wouldn't realise it, it would be no punishment if he commanded her to remain in her room all evening.

'Very well,' he snapped, but instead of leaving and ordering her to miss dinner, to Julia's horror he immediately locked the bedroom door and grabbed hold of her. Almost before she knew what was happening, owing to the swiftness of his movements and the strength of his arms, she found her black dress unzipped and flung in a heap across the floor.

'What do you think you're doing?' she cried wildly, beginning to struggle frantically as she recovered her breath and realised she was standing in nothing but her bra and a pair of silky panties.

'Wait and see,' he rasped.

'If you don't let go of me, I'll scream!' she choked furiously.

'Go ahead,' he snapped, his voice still tight with anger as he thrust her ruthlessly down before the wall mounted vanity mirror, 'but I'd advise you to save your strength for later. You may need it!'

CHAPTER FOUR

THE edge of the stool she was sitting on began hurting the backs of Julia's legs, bringing from her a humiliating whimper instead of the furious comments that were going through her mind as she tried to escape the iron grip of Guy's hands. As he stood behind her, holding her against him until her first defiance subsided, she thought her shape must be imprinted on every hard muscle in his body. The arm he had round her rose slowly to graze her half-covered breasts, sending a curious sensation spinning through her as it came up to allow him to grasp a handful of her long, thick hair. When she moved again, in one last endeavour to break free of him, his grip tightened, bringing a pain so intense she immediately sat still.

'Had enough?' he bit out.

Closing her eyes in silent appeal, she knew she was powerless against his superior strength and the suffocating rioting of her senses that was washing away all her resistance. When miserably she nodded, she expected him to release her, but to her dismay he merely reached for a pot of cold cream and began slapping it on her face.

'This should soon do the trick,' he muttered harshly.

'I could manage myself!' she spluttered sullenly, having enough sense left to know when she was beaten. If she didn't give in she was sure her hair would soon be out by the roots!

He didn't trust her. 'I've started so I'll finish, as one of your famous TV personalities is fond of saying,' he rasped. 'I never leave a job half done.'

'Killing me won't achieve anything!' she retorted

hoarsely, too aware now of the hard muscular arms forcing her to him, holding her totally captive.

'I don't intend going as far as that,' he replied coldly, while the pressure of his hands seemed to imply that he might like to.

Violence returned to Julia. There was an element about him she couldn't explain, an air of superiority clearly expressing his belief that there wasn't a woman alive he couldn't deal with. And already, she admitted, the restraint he placed on her was making itself felt. Invective words hovered on the end of her tongue, yet she couldn't get one of them out, and her hands and arms, which longed to hit him with every ounce of her strength, appeared to be pinned at her sides.

'Are you quite finished?' was the best she could manage after a long pause.

'Patience,' he advised, beginning to remove the layers of cream with a tissue until her face was almost clean. 'This is only the first stage.'

Before she could ask what he meant, he increased her frozen apprehension further by lifting her swiftly over to the bathroom and dumping her unceremoniously into the shower unit. While she struggled to regain both her breath and her balance, needles of warm water began spraying over her, soaking her hair, streaming over her body as she steadied herself. Over her hair Guy tipped a generous measure of shampoo, rubbing it ruthlessly into her scalp, taking no notice of her anguished pleas when some of the soap got in her eyes, making them smart so much she couldn't see.

'Guy!' she choked furiously, feeling she was drowning as he rinsed and soaped and rinsed again. His thoroughness rendered her helpless, the turmoil was all in her mind.

'Save your fury for another time, *mon enfant*,' he grunted. 'I am generating more than enough for the two of us.'

'You'll pay for this!' she spluttered unheeding.

The contempt on his face might have shown her what he thought of her threats if she had been able to see it, but she heard enough from the one or two things he muttered under his breath to gather that he wasn't impressed. Again without warning he lifted her, this time out of the shower.

Her threshing arms were humiliatingly ineffective as he ducked neatly. With all the ease of an experienced combatant he seized her wet hair in a huge towel, roughly drying it while water streamed from the rest of her on to the floor. In the struggle in the shower one strap of her bra must have snapped, showing more of her figure than she deemed decent.

'Look at me!' she half screamed, her cheeks on fire.

'Is that an invitation?'

To her consternation, his hands paused to allow his glance to sweep over her cynically. 'Oh!' She was so disconcerted, so incredibly mixed up she scarcely knew what she was either doing or saying, but provocation was the last thing on her mind. Catching sight of herself in the wall mirror, she shuddered with mounting horror, The opalescent gleam of her soft curves was more than a mere invitation, it was almost a demand to be ravished. Her breasts might have been bare beneath the wet transparency of her clinging bra, and below them her tiny waist and slender, curved hips looked so sinuous as to arouse excitement. For a moment she imagined she caught a glimpse of something very like excitement in Guy's darkening eyes, and because a similar emotion stirred within her, she felt ready to sink through the floor with shame.

'Let me go!' she moaned, through shaking lips. 'What will people think?'

'Don't worry.' In a flash, his expression was washed clean of everything but extreme coldness. 'No one will see you like this but me. In any case, nudity in warm climates fails to incite much interest.'

Once more his glance ran over her briefly, then

returned to her face. A short silence followed as their eyes caught and held. Despite his dismissive comment, she felt the tension in the atmosphere, and there was suddenly a dazed expression in her face as something inside her began flaring like the rush of spray from a switched-on fountain. Only, whatever it was, there was none of a fountain's coolness. It more resembled water on a fire slowly increasing in heat until it scalded. When Guy's glance touched her she found herself responding without knowing what was happening to her. The only thing which registered, that she might describe, was the sudden smouldering of his eyes, his deepening breathing, the dull red colour creeping under the hard skin of his cheeks.

'Guy?' she whispered, a certain vein of helplessness and vulnerability in the pallor of her face and softly parted lips.

Slowly his head bent until his lips were brushing hers. He touched her so lightly that she wasn't prepared for the shock of electricity that flashed through her, flicking every raw nerve unbearably, making her cry out.

Immediately he withdrew with a sharp exclamation, looking so impatient she began believing she had only dreamt he had been kissing her. 'You have to hurry. *Mon Dieu*, must every woman entice!' Almost savagely he thrust the towel which he had been using on her hair around her bare shoulders, as if to hide the sight of her, and his voice was not amused.

Swiftly he found a brush, wielding it on her heavy tangled head, her gasps of undisguised pain seeming to afford him a kind of grim pleasure. When he switched on the nearby drier she was past struggling. Somehow the pain he was causing only made her long to feel his mouth on hers again, and she wondered how long it would be, if ever, before he would kiss her properly, as he had done on the day he had taken her out.

He might have guessed the tumultuous thoughts

occupying her mind, for he continued to be far from
gentle. As soon as he finished with her hair, he dragged
her across the bedroom, halting in front of her
wardrobe which he flung open. 'Now,' he grated,
removing a soft white dress from its hanger, 'this one, I
think.'

Because it was her favourite, she had to defy him.
'I'm supposed to be in mourning!'

'This is exactly right for a young girl in such
circumstances,' he said adamantly, 'sad and virginal.'

'Yet you're thrusting me at young men!'

'Not into bed with them.'

'Would you care if I went as far as that?' she
challenged, a knot of misery and anger in her throat,
'Then they might have to marry me.'

His face went curiously pale but none the less
unrelenting. 'You certainly won't have to go that far.'

'Won't I?'

'Tiens!' his dark eyes hardened at the defiant gleam in
hers. 'Can't you stop talking drivel and get into this?'
Leaving the dress in her arms, he turned abruptly to
jerk open a drawer and throw a handful of fresh undies
on her bed. 'That's everything you need, so get a move
on!'

Julia's glance explored the shower of silk on her
counterpane. Guy's hands had moved like lightning, at
random, but everything was there. Involuntarily her
hands clutched tighter on her enveloping towel. 'You
must have had some practice, *monsieur*. Does Lorraine
appreciate such expertise?'

His mouth tightened. 'Lorraine doesn't provoke me
at all.'

'Just sleeps with you.'

'Dieu!'

As he appeared ready to do her bodily harm, Julia
realised she had gone too far—and yet ... 'Well,' she
lifted mutinous shoulders, 'I know you're going to be
married, so why not?'

For a moment, as he stepped towards her, his hands curled to white-knuckled fists, she felt really frightened. The relief she felt when he paused on a harshly drawn breath made her tremble. His voice was almost normal when he snapped icily, 'You know more than is good for you, *mon enfant*. Now, do you intend dressing yourself or do you want me to help you?'

'Oh, no!' Clutching her dress in one hand, she scooped her other things off her bed with the other. As she fled to the bathroom, where she had suffered such humiliation, she cried wildly, 'You may have won this time, *monsieur*, but you won't always!'

Five minutes later she returned, clad modestly in pale cotton and lace, her hair falling, with only its natural wave, over her shoulders. Her face, devoid of make-up, apart from the merest gloss of pale pink lipstick, revealed a pureness of bone and skin which might have delighted the heart of even the most insensitive artist. Julia, however, was sure she looked insipid and colourless, and although she preferred her skin without cosmetics there were occasions, she believed, when they were necessary.

'Will I do?' she asked, almost belligerently, daring him to complain again.

Guy had been watching her closely, now he looked away and she saw a muscle twitch in his cheek. Thinking she had angered him again, she awaited his verdict uncertainly.

'You'll do,' he said shortly.

'Guy,' she came nearer, attempting to steady her voice as she promised, 'I'll try to behave myself.' Her heart beating over-fast, she hesitated, wondering what more she could say. He couldn't expect complete capitulation, could he? Resentment couldn't be got rid of that easily, but she considered, after all his rough treatment, that it was very generous of her to meet him more than half way. 'I'll try to be good,' she repeated, feeling the essence of martyrdom as she paused beside him.

He nodded, his slight smile revealing nothing as he turned back to her and lifted his hand to her still damp hair. Changing the subject completely, he murmured, 'This will prove an excuse for being late. Your hair is too thick to dry easily by normal methods.'

Avoiding his eyes, she stared at his wet shirt clinging to his tautly muscled chest. His whole body was clad in tightly packed muscle. He looked lean, but he wasn't, it was just that he carried no surplus flesh. Feeling her glance sliding, Julia shivered, jerking it upright again.

'If—when I meet your guests,' she stammered unhappily, 'I will be polite to them, but I—well,' she muttered, 'I haven't honestly had any experience with men. You'll have to make allowances if I appear slow and awkward.'

'Don't sound so desperate, Julia.' He sounded faintly amused. 'Just be your natural self and I don't think you'll have any complaints.'

She looked at him suspiciously, then gave up. One could never tell exactly what Guy was thinking. 'Are you coming down with me?'

'Of course.' The sardonic gleam faded from his eyes to be replaced by a brief intentness as they rested on where her small white teeth caught nervously on her dewy bottom lip. 'But as I've just told you, there's no need to panic. If you like you can come with me now and wait while I change my shirt. I shan't be many minutes.'

Julia wished she had waited where she was as she hovered outside his bedroom door and caught a glimpse of the huge bed he slept in. Had Lorraine ever slept there? she wondered. Owls weren't the only things to wander at night!

'Come along.' Guy was back with her, cutting through her suddenly torturous thoughts, propelling her before him, so autocratic in his dark suit that she found herself trembling.

The guests were arriving as they went downstairs. Somehow Julia felt it was Guy and she who were making an entrance as several pairs of eyes turned to watch their descent of the long staircase. Guy had his hand under her arm in a firm grip, taking no chances of her nerves overwhelming her at the last moment and trying to escape him. It was a warder and prisoner situation, but, Julia realised, catching a glimpse of the black rage on Lorraine's upturned face, it could be construed differently. At the bottom of the stairs, her heart beating too loudly from such an intimate contact with him, she attempted to pull her arm from his grasp.

She was sure, if they had been alone, he might have laughed at her futile struggles. He introduced her to everyone before he allowed her to go. Why was it, she thought despairingly, that his very glance was magnetic, pinning her against her will but quite as effectively as chains to his side?

'Behave yourself!' came his curt whisper, as he left her talking to a middle-aged couple, completely ignoring the mute appeal in her eyes.

It amazed Julia how he kept what she could only describe as a proprietorial eye on her all evening while managing to act the superb host to a great many people. Not that there were that many, a dozen or so at the most, but she had grown used to the small family circle and this evening, although there was an abundance of room, to her the *salons* and terraces seemed overcrowded.

There were only four people there in the same age group as herself, and two of these were girls. The boys were a few years older. One of these was the son of a charming couple who owned a vineyard, fifty miles away, but it was the other young man, Pierre Boutin, who pursued her the more diligently. Julia couldn't make her mind up about him. He was pleasant but rather pompous, like his parents, and she found his constant hints regarding his father's wealth slightly irritating. The importance of his own position didn't go unmentioned either.

'One day, *mademoiselle*,' he informed her, 'my father's estates will come to me.'

'How nice,' she answered.

'I think so,' he didn't appear to notice her lack of enthusiasm. 'Naturally I have been brought up to appreciate everything I will inherit. Even our house which is full of precious things is sacred to me.'

'Really?' Julia was quite at loss to know what else to say. Pierre Boutin was an enigma, she wasn't quite sure what to make of him. She couldn't believe he was typical of the average young Frenchman, he was too solemn. No doubt he was very proper and well-behaved, but somehow she felt it might be difficult even to like him, let alone love him.

Guy wasn't far away and she was aware of his narrow-eyed attention even as he talked to his other guests, who, she noticed mutinously, didn't appear to be half as boring as Pierre. She tried to be fair. People were the same the world over, she supposed. All society had its quota of bores—it was just unfortunate she was landed with one!

Pierre's mother, after whom he had obviously taken, looked on Julia suspiciously, but in much the same way as she viewed the other young women who approached him. Even so, Julia was somewhat startled, the next morning, when Guy told her that Madame Boutin had been favourably impressed.

'You won't forget she has asked you for tea?'

'Would you let me?' The face Julia turned to him was flawless in the searching rays of sunlight. 'I accepted anyway.'

'Only when prompted.'

Did he have to remind her of his hand prodding her back, of his breath mingling with hers as he had taken it upon himself to assure a departing Madame Boutin she would be delighted and Julia had turned to him with an indignant, if futile gasp? Their eyes had met, Guy's intent, harshly insistent, hers oddly dilated. It had been a few seconds out of time when the others, for Julia, had ceased to exist. Vaguely she had been aware of curious, veiled glances and again of Lorraine's fury, but the only thing which had really registered was of something mysteriously inexplicable passing between Guy and herself.

'I'm not entirely helpless,' she remonstrated now, her face tinged with colour because of what she recalled. She had an unhappy feeling that Guy knew he could render her helpless and enjoyed doing so.

'You needed a little help,' he said soothingly.

Her eyes lifted to the squarish, deeply cleft chin, the hard, sensuous face, and Pierre Boutin's image fled. She began to speak, but as though anticipating the protests she was about to utter, he placed a lightly admonitory finger on her lips. As the shock of his touch ran through her, holding her momentarily still, his finger began moving, as if under its own compulsion over the full, yielding softness of her mouth. She wasn't aware how she seemed to have stopped breathing for fear of interrupting him as his finger traversed her mouth like a kiss.

From nearby the harsh croak of a raven released her from the trance she was in. Jerking her head back, so Guy's hand fell away, she spoke with an effort, 'I—I don't really want to go.'

'But you will.'

She watched his hands being thrust in his pockets and a look of cruel determination sweep any tenderness from his expression. 'How do I get there?' she asked helplessly.

'I'll drive you.'

Wasn't he doing it all the time! 'You will?'

'Yes. Haven't you realised yet, *mon enfant*,' he added suavely, 'how willing I am to help you when you don't defy me?'

Despite his promise, Julia hadn't believed he would take her, but when the day arrived he did. Nor did she expect her visit to go so smoothly but it did. The Boutins' home, as Pierre had assured her, was filled with beautiful things, so many of them obviously priceless that when shown around them Julia was almost too nervous to breathe.

On her second visit, sandwiched between several which Pierre paid her, she went alone, driving the small car which Guy had put at her disposal. As it was a distance of only ten miles, though the roads weren't so good, it didn't take long. Privately, although she continued seeing Pierre to please Guy, she didn't feel their relationship was getting anywhere. Sometimes, in the privacy of her room, she giggled about it, other times she almost wept. From the way he was going about things, she suspected Pierre might be thinking seriously of asking her to be his wife. He droned on so continuously about his assets and expectations that he could only be leading up to a proposal. Obviously, by painting as dazzling a picture of his wealth as possible, he was making sure that Julia would find it impossible to refuse him.

Aunt Mavis had said very little about Pierre's growing attachment to her niece. The only comment she had allowed herself, when once Julia had wondered why Pierre wasn't already married, was that a girl he had been engaged to earlier had died and since then his parents hadn't found anyone to please him. 'But,' she had added approvingly, 'whoever he marries won't lack for material things.'

As Pierre didn't mention his late fiancée, Julia didn't say anything herself. She felt neither curious or jealous, which must prove, she decided, that she couldn't be in love with him. This small piece of self-knowledge, however, she kept to herself. If Guy should learn that she would certainly reject Pierre for this reason, she could guess how angry he would be!

Pierre was out when she arrived, but his mother was waiting for her. Her son wouldn't be long, she said importantly, he was dealing with an unexpected emergency on the estate.

On this, their third meeting, Madame Boutin began taking more notice of Julia. She began thawing visibly. After coffee, with Pierre still absent, she allowed Julia to see her remarkable collection of centuries-old porcelain and glass.

'Has Guy shown you his collection?' Madame Boutin asked, and when Julia shook her head, 'His mother, Yves' first wife, was a contemporary of mine, and, although she hadn't quite my enthusiasm she left him many beautiful things. There is a pitcher you must see, from Kashan, painted in underglaze blue, dated about A.D. 1200. I would give a lot to possess it.'

'Maman must like you,' Pierre said later.

'What makes you think so?' Julia asked idly.

He frowned a little at her careless tone. 'Not every girl is allowed to see her treasures.'

Julia suspected Madame Boutin had wafted her away in order to provide herself with a golden opportunity to ask Julia several searching questions about her parents. And Madame's inquisitiveness, much as she had tried to disguise it, had struck a discordant note. Julia had felt she was being more astute than sympathetic and had consequently answered stiffly, giving little away. She didn't mention any of this to Pierre though. Instead she merely murmured noncommittally, 'I see.'

Pierre, she soon discovered, was as dull as he was pompous and, like his mother, appeared entirely without a sense of humour. Julia knew she could never marry a man incapable of laughing at himself occasionally, no matter what Guy said!

She didn't see much of Guy these days, perhaps because she did her best to avoid him, but when, for a while, he had to be away on business she missed him dreadfully. She puzzled over this, because she was still

smarting because of the way he had made her change
her dress, the night of the dinner party, and she had
thought his absence would act like a balm on her
wounded spirits. Contrarily the period during which he
was gone stretched like a lifetime and she hadn't dared
try to analyse her feelings. She had thrown herself
instead into a frenzy of activity with the twins and
concentrated on her riding lessons and getting to know
the men better.

Guy didn't actually push her friendship with Pierre,
although he continued to approve of it. If he noticed
she refused to go out with Pierre alone he didn't say
anything, and she went on accepting only invitations
which included other young people. She wouldn't
have hesitated if Guy had asked her anywhere, she
confessed to herself, watching wistfully one evening as
he escorted a clinging Lorraine around the garden
until the falling darkness hid them from sight.
Lorraine was looking radiant, just now, and more
triumphant as the days passed, and she revelled in
Guy's increasing attention. Julia considered it might
be just a matter of time before an important
announcement was made, and she realised, as if
struck by lightning, that when that happened she
wouldn't be able to stay in France.

Again she refused to face the reason why she should
feel so devastated at the thought of Lorraine being
Guy's wife, but the tension that grew inside her as she
waited for such an announcement began affecting her
appetite so that she lost weight. When this became
apparent and her healthy colour began to fade, Guy
called her to his office after dinner, one night.

'You're losing weight again,' he said sternly, waving
her to a chair.

Julia hadn't wanted to sit down as this seemed to
indicate a long session with him, something she tried to
avoid, but when he fixed her with that look in his eyes
she found she couldn't defy him.

'It could be love, *monsieur*,' she was aghast to hear herself saying, yet knowing suddenly and hopelessly that she was only speaking the truth. That it wasn't Pierre she loved, she couldn't explain, although that was the conclusion she was sure Guy would jump to.

Quite obviously he did, and he seemed startled, yet not in the way she had vaguely anticipated. The ensuing silence caused her discreetly lowered lids to fly up again, and she was surprised to see how pale he had gone. Surely he couldn't be as relieved as all that?

'You're sure you're in love?' he asked curtly, without expression, as if he had suddenly become aware of her staring at him.

'I think so,' she replied hollowly, wishing feverishly that she had been able to deny it.

'A young girl's emotions are never very stable,' he commented tonelessly, his face curiously set.

Something about him she couldn't define tempted Julia to say, 'And if I believe mine are?'

He drew a harsh breath, almost a sigh of resignation. 'Pierre is a very commendable young man and if you feel you care for him deeply, I don't think you could do better.'

Indeed! Anger flared in Julia's breast. What kind of opinion did Guy have of her, to judge that she should be honoured that someone like Pierre should stoop to offer her his name?

'He's pompous!' she retorted, furiously letting her tongue run away with her when she had intended goading him by pretending to admire Pierre. Now she realised the futility of such a course. How could she have, even unconsciously, presumed she might taunt Guy as if he was a jealous lover? He would never be her lover, much as she might secretly yearn for him.

'Pierre,' he frowned, obviously thinking, if nothing else, she was extremely mixed up, 'pompous?'

'So's his mother!' Despairing rage drove her unwarily, her grey eyes flashing in foolish defiance at

Guy's raised brows, 'The house is filled with stupid bric-à-brac, which would be better given to charity. One scarcely dares breathe for fear of damaging anything. Madame Boutin even hints that the carpets should be looked at rather than trodden on, and . . .'

'That's enough, Julia!' Guy's voice was a whiplash, driving colour wildly to her cheeks. 'Madame Boutin's collections are famous and not to be sneered at.'

'I wasn't sneering!'

'The impression I received . . .'

'Oh, damn your impressions!'

'Julia!' This time his anger wasn't concealed. It leapt darkly from his blue eyes, hardening the lines about his mouth formidably.

Julia's face went white. She seldom if ever used words like that, and never in that tone. She reacted to him like no one else, but how could she tell him? 'I'm sorry,' she mumbled.

He left his chair to grasp her shoulders, dragging her up beside him, looking as if he could happily have shaken the life out of her. 'One thing I will not tolerate is insolence!'

She could feel his breath on her face, but it was something she was growing curiously addicted to. 'I said the wrong thing?'

'It wasn't only what you said, it was the look in your eyes.'

His hands were hurting her shoulders and seemed to be drawing her closer. 'I can't help it if I don't like Pierre's home,' she muttered, hardly able to think of Pierre at all.

'If you love him you must try to,' Guy retorted grimly. 'Remember, whoever you marry in France, you must learn to tolerate his relatives.'

'Lorraine won't tolerate yours!' Julia returned sharply. 'Me, for instance—she hates me!'

'You aren't really a relative.'

'No,' something sounding suspiciously like a sob

escaped her as she lowered her head, 'I'm not really anything am I?'

He went very still, but his face was once more sardonic. 'You're a crazy, mixed-up juvenile with an outsize imagination. One day you're going to be quite something. And we're all very fond of you.'

Julia was about to snap, 'How nice!' until she raised her eyes and met his staring down on her intently. Somehow the words died in her throat along with her wits, and without meaning to, or being conscious of what she might be divulging, she murmured, 'It's not only Pierre's house. I like you much better than I like him.'

'You just told me you loved him!' His voice was low but none the less emphatic.

Julia bit her lips to stop it trembling. What a mess she was making of everything! In another second, if she wasn't careful, he would have her confessing who it was she really loved! 'I made a mistake,' she faltered.

'A mistake?'

She tried to disregard the contempt in his tones. 'What I mean is—well, I told you I wasn't sure,' she reiterated huskily, feeling cornered. 'Haven't you ever had doubts about—well, being in love?'

'No!' he snapped. 'Personally, I don't believe in it.'

'Oh,' her face paled again. 'So when you marry it will be a business arrangement?'

'It could be,' he agreed coldly, 'but a marriage is entirely different from a business. And one doesn't need to be in love to make love, which is one of the most pleasurable things in the world.'

'How would I know?' Misery gnawed at Julia's heart as she unconsciously gave all her secrets away, 'I suppose I'd better stick to Pierre, if he wants me. He must be more in my league.'

'Yes. Go on?' he taunted.

'At least he—he's a gentleman, not like you!' she gulped. 'He hasn't mauled me about. He hasn't even tried to kiss me yet!' She hadn't given him the chance, but Guy wasn't to know.

Anger hardened Guy's mouth so that when it hit hers she would have cried with pain, had she been able to. He loosened the grip of one hand from her shoulders to clasp her face, turning her mouth up to meet his. She could feel the anger behind his driving kiss, as if he was determined to exchange insult for insult. For a moment all she could feel was pain as her lips were ground under his and the harsh rise and fall of his chest against her breasts hurt excruciatingly. But when she tried instinctively to get away he merely tightened his hold on her.

Julia went limp against him, willing her mind to blot out the feel of his rugged strength. There was no tenderness in his kiss, no gentle persuasion, yet she felt herself sliding into a euphoria of mutual desire. As Guy eased the iron pressure of his arms slightly, she became acutely aware of him, of his hand wandering down her throat, burning her skin like a brand moving across her body. An incredible sweetness spread through her as she was suspended in time and space, unable to respond to anything other than his mouth moving expertly over her own.

She was conscious of the same deep stirring in her stomach and limbs that she had felt when he had kissed her in the truck, and unknowingly she gasped and shivered. As a low moan escaped her his body seemed to shudder in unison, then, as swiftly as he had taken hold of her, he was pushing her away.

Feeling his arms leaving her, she opened her eyes to find some distance between them but still a peculiar air of tension. 'You hurt me!' she whispered, the tips of her fingers touching bruised lips.

The broad shoulders straightened as his sensuous mouth hardened. 'Now I might admit you have something to complain of, but I don't usually go in for kissing girls of your age unless provoked. It might pay you to remember.'

'An excuse . . .!'

'*Mademoiselle*, watch your words! I believe I've already told you, I never look for an excuse to justify my actions. When a girl arouses a man's anger he frequently resorts to one of two things—either shaking or kissing her.'

'You did both.'

His eyes glinted coldly. 'Then you can decide which form of chastisement you like best and next time state your preference.'

If he intended shocking her slightly, which Julia felt intuitively he did, he was certainly succeeding! Yet she knew miserably that she would have braved his anger a second time if he would kiss her again. The touch of his mouth seemed imprinted on her mind as well as her lips and aroused in her body an increasing if bewildering hunger.

'You're being outrageous!' she retorted sharply, determined to destroy the crazy inclinations consuming her. 'I'm sure I don't provoke you very often, and never intentionally.'

'You're probably right,' he began looking bored, 'the issue has perhaps got rather out of hand. I suggest, Julia, that while you would do worse than to consider Pierre's suit seriously, there is no rush. I shouldn't like you to feel we want to get rid of you immediately.'

CHAPTER FIVE

THE next few days brought a minor crisis to the family which helped surprisingly to break through Julia's increasing despair. For a little while, at any rate, it took her mind off her own troubles. Her cousin Fayme, who was pregnant again, became ill after returning from Germany and was unable to come and collect the twins. As her doctor had ordered complete rest, the twins were to stay with their grandmother for the time being. All this, Fayme's husband came personally to tell them, having decided a telephone message might prove too upsetting for Mavis.

Léon Pacquet was a pleasant man, getting on in years. Julia had somehow imagined he would be younger. 'We never thought this would happen,' he said wryly. 'For years we've hoped for another child and were delighted when at last our wish was granted. I allowed Fayme to come to Germany with me,' he explained, when Guy remarked shortly that she might have been better at home, 'because, ironically I thought it would give her a rest. However,' he admitted heavily, 'it didn't work out that way. She didn't like being alone and began running around too much, although her doctor doesn't believe that was entirely responsible for her complications.'

He had been happier when he had left, after Lorraine had assured him she would stay with the twins and look after them as she had been doing. Julia, almost bursting with indignation, had scarcely been able to prevent herself from telling him who had really been looking after them, but to do so might only have given the impression that she objected to the extra work. As she loved the twins and enjoyed their company, this was the last thing she wanted anyone to think, but Lorraine's arrogance sometimes made her see red. With Lorraine's presence ensured for possibly another few weeks, to say nothing of the probability of her engagement to Guy being announced, Julia was sometimes tempted to encourage Pierre much more than she did.

Everything was going Lorraine's way, she thought unhappily, one afternoon as she wandered around the house with the twins. Aunt Mavis frequently wanted first-hand information of her daughter's progress under some new treatment she was having, and as she was unable to travel herself she appeared grateful when Lorraine offered to go instead, if Guy would drive her. Julia envied her the times she set out with him. It usually took them all day and Lorraine nearly always returned looking extremely satisfied.

Yesterday had been one of the days when they had visited Fayme, and today Lorraine was resting in her room with another of her headaches. The weather had turned surprisingly stormy, forcing Julia and the two boys indoors, a circumstance none of them appreciated. Julia followed the twins abstractedly. Mavis had mentioned that Pierre and his mother were coming for tea, and she wasn't looking forward to it. If the weather had been better she could have stayed outside and perhaps pretended to have forgotten about it until after they had gone. Pierre was often at his most boring when his mother was around; he seemed to feel duty bound to defer to her before he either moved or spoke.

The twins, taking advantage of the fact that Julia's attention was elsewhere, led her unwittingly to one of the little-used *salons*. They knew they weren't supposed to be there, but they loved exploring, especially when the grown-up with them didn't say no. It wasn't a very comfortable room, being furnished with stiff period chairs and sofas, gilt-edged and unyielding, and only one rug on the hard polished floor. Around the walls stood elaborate glass cases on spindly legs containing valuable ornaments of porcelain and glass. Although she hadn't been here before, Julia remembered Mavis pointing it out to her one day. It had been the favourite *salon* of Guy's mother and, as such, had been left exactly as it was when she died. Mavis had opened the door and given her a glimpse of a fine French ormolu clock flanked on either side by a pair of Louise Seize ormolu and bronze candelabra, and for Julia it had been enough. Despite Mavis's assurance that she was welcome to have a good look round if she wished, she had been reluctant to do so without Guy's permission. Without it she had known she would feel as if she was trespassing.

She was annoyed with herself now for not taking more notice of where the twins were going, but as it was her fault they were here she hadn't the heart to drag them out immediately. They weren't actually touching anything, just looking. Warning them to be good, she only intended giving them another few minutes, when her attention was caught by a nineteenth-century French painting by Jean Cazin. Something about it stirred her imagination. She knew little of art in any form, but suddenly she realised she would like to. Guy was quite an authority, though he rode most of the day with his men out on the salt marshes, dressed as roughly as any of them. He might be willing to teach her if she could explain her sudden peculiar hunger to learn.

So absorbed was she that she really did jump with alarm on hearing the door of one of the cabinets being flung open and Fortune's piping voice exclaiming, 'Ooh! this is *Oncle* Guy's favourite!'

Julia had believed the cabinets to be locked and she was frozen with horror as Fortune removed a beautifully painted Royal Worcester pot-pourri vase and began waving it about. And before she could either speak or reach him he had dropped it. To her consternation it seemed to slip through his hot little fingers in a flash, hitting the hard floor with a crash.

'Oh, Fortune!' she wailed loudly, as both boys fled to the other side of the room. 'What am I to do?' she cried, stumbling to her knees beside the broken vase and beginning to pick up the pieces before chastising the twins. If the vase was one Guy was particularly fond of then heaven help the poor lambs!

'Julia?' As though thinking of him had caused him to materialise in person, Guy's voice from the doorway made Julia jump again. With Pierre and his mother ranged on either side of him against the huge double doors, she felt worse than if she'd been faced with a platoon of enemy soldiers. 'What on earth's been going on?' he rasped, as she made a futile attempt to hide the fragments of china from him.

'I . . .' she began, only to be cut off harshly as he advanced farther into the room and clearly saw what had happened. '*Mon Dieu!*' he snapped, 'have you any idea what that piece was worth?'

Julia cast a frantic glance at the obviously quaking twins huddled against the window. She could actually see the fear in their faces. With their mother ill how could she make their lot worse? They'd had to be told about their mother—there had been no other way to explain her prolonged absence—and Julia knew they were secretly fretting. If Guy was to learn who had really been responsible for the breakage, there was no knowing what form his anger might take, and she knew she couldn't betray them.

'I—I'm sorry,' she whispered, staring down at the damage, realising the hopelessness of offering to pay for it. She had no money, not even a job. All she could do was pretend to be full of remorse, and she didn't have to pretend very hard. She did feel full of remorse that something so beautiful had been broken, and in a way she was responsible. Instead of feeling sorry for herself, she ought to have been watching what the twins were doing and never let them in here! The least she could do now was to try and divert

Guy's attention from them until Fortune stopped looking so guilty.

Guy was regarding her with tightening mouth and glittering eyes, but he was looking at her white face rather than at the broken vase. It was Madame Boutin who broke the fraught silence following Julia's faltering words.

'Such careless stupidity!' she gasped. 'If this girl had been of less consequence, Guy, I'd have advised you to pack her off immediately!'

Pierre, appearing completely stunned, echoed his mother incredulously. 'Few French girls would be so irresponsible, Maman.'

'Imagine her,' Madame's horrified gaze flickered from her son to Julia, 'among my precious things!'

Pierre nodded in apprehensive agreement, clearly stricken.

Guy suddenly intervened, as if he had had enough. 'If you would conduct your mother to the other *salon*,' he said to Pierre, 'I'll deal with this.'

Madame Boutin wasn't to be removed so easily. She settled in the doorway like an enormous black frog, fixing Julia with a malevolent eye. 'But this is terrible!' she reiterated excitedly. 'You understand, Guy, I wouldn't dare let this girl in my house again. I couldn't take the risk!'

'Please!' Guy begged stiffly.

'I'm sorry, Guy,' Madame replied in a similar manner. 'As you must know, I would never ordinarily insult one of your guests, but this is no ordinary circumstance and I feel very upset. So much so,' she finished haughtily, 'that I don't feel able to stay for tea. Please present my apologies to your dear stepmother. Come, Pierre!'

Julia trembled as Madame Boutin swept from their sight, Pierre following like an obedient puppy. Guy, with an exasperated sigh, went after them, but five minutes later he was back. In his absence, she had sent the twins away, but was still on her knees trying to tidy up.

'Leave it,' he snapped, 'and go to your room.'

He was still angry, although he appeared to have himself well under control, but she refused to be dismissed like a naughty child.

'Have they really gone?' she asked nervously.

'What would you expect?'

Swallowing hard, Julia went on blindly picking up pieces. 'I would have done anything to prevent this happening.'

'I'd rather not hear any more,' he retorted tersely, his eyes meeting hers icily as he dragged her to her feet. 'You can take it you won't be seeing Pierre again, but next time you feel like getting rid of a suitor, I'd appreciate it if you tried a less expensive method!'

'You don't mean . . .' Julia couldn't have felt worse if he had struck her. How could he believe she would stoop so low, be ruthless enough to sink to such deviousness? Madame Boutin, being what she was—and with her fanatical regard for antiques, might be excused for being unpleasant, but Julia felt she could never forgive Guy. Never! 'You're completely wrong and insulting!' she cried. 'I wasn't even thinking of Pierre!'

Guy didn't bother to argue. With a shrug of disdain, he glanced at the broken vase and told her to get out of his sight, and this time, sick at heart, she obeyed him.

Although she realised she had only herself to blame that he should think the worst of her, it didn't help to make her feel less miserable. It seemed to Julia that if he had bothered to study her character at all, he would have known she wasn't capable of such intrigue and wouldn't have condemned her so quickly. She couldn't forget how he had looked at her, the utter contempt in his eyes, and she hadn't thought it possible to feel so unhappy.

It soon became obvious, in the following days, that

Guy now had no time for her, as he left her severely alone. It was the way he ignored her that hurt most. Not even his worst tirades, she came to acknowledge, had been as hard to endure as his apparent willingness to pretend she just didn't exist.

For a while after the incident of the vase, the twins had been strangely quiet, but not long enough for anyone to wonder about it. Mavis liked to think they missed their mother, and, while she sympathised, she approved rather than questioned.

Mavis only mentioned the vase to Julia briefly and without referring to either Pierre or his mother she said she was sure it had been an accident and that Julia mustn't fret over it.

'Guy has secured the door of the *salon*,' she told Julia gently. 'Now no one can be tempted to wander in. The maids have a habit of forgetting to lock the cabinets after dusting. From now on, Hortense will do it herself.'

Although eventually Guy's manner returned almost to normal, there remained a certain coolness which Julia found hard to bear. She missed having him stop to talk to her, as he had frequently done, even in the middle of one of his busiest days, and she sighed over vague, indefinable dreams which could now never come to fruition.

She was startled when he sought her out, one morning in the stables. She was there alone, talking to one of the horses. The animal was suffering from a slight malady and was being kept inside until he was better. When his companions were out working, Julia often came to see him as she guessed he would be lonely and perhaps as unsettled as herself.

Guy, halting beside her, ran his eyes expertly over the horse while he told Julia that Pierre and his mother had left to visit friends in Brittany, and from there were going on to Paris.

As his eyes left the horse to study her face, Julia realised instinctively that he had mentioned this deliberately in order to observe her reactions. How was she supposed to react? she wondered uneasily. Suddenly she wanted to please him desperately, if only to get back on their previous footing, and if this meant having to pretend a little, she didn't care.

Cautiously she remarked, 'I hope they have a good time.'

She mustn't have said the right thing, for he frowned. 'Does that remark have any particular significance?'

Julia shook her head, trying not to look to where his shirt was open to the waist, exposing a wealth of thick, dark body hair curling over his broad chest. Slightly apprehensive, as his mouth tightened, she whispered, 'Should it?'

This time he sighed impatiently. 'I thought you were growing fond of Pierre, despite his mother, but it appears your heart might be made of stone.'

'At my age?'

'This,' he grated, 'is what I don't understand. There's nothing wrong with your heart, you're a normal young girl, and I believed you might be heartbroken when Pierre defected so easily.'

'Why, you're as pompous as he is!' Julia exclaimed angrily, 'and as ready to condemn me! I was never in love with Pierre, if that's what you're getting at?' Recklessly she added, 'I never even let him kiss me!'

For a moment Guy's taut jaw appeared to relax, although his eyes still smouldered. 'You can call me anything you like, but not pompous.'

That hadn't been fair, but it had caught him on the raw, something she hadn't thought possible. Or, if it was, that he would deign to protest. 'I'm sorry,' she muttered, only half meaning it.

Menacingly he hit back. 'If you had allowed Pierre more licence, a little more encouragement, instead of ignoring him half the time, you might have discovered you could respond to him. I've found no lack of response whenever I've kissed you.'

How like him to be able to discuss this so coolly! But if it was no holds barred, she could play that way herself! 'Perhaps you always choose a vulnerable moment, *monsieur*. I wouldn't normally respond to someone like you. Another time—if there is another time—you might warn me, then I would be prepared.'

Instead of subduing him, her flushed face and thready voice appeared to afford him a kind of caustic amusement. 'You mean you have defences you might erect?'

Julia swallowed hard, looking down at the stable floor. How had such a conversation ever got started? It was dangerous—how dangerous she needed no one to tell her. Guy was waiting, like a cat waits for a mouse to make a move, then he would pounce. She knew that by agreeing she was playing right into his hands, but what alternative did she have?

'Yes!' she retorted defiantly.

With the glint deepening in his eyes, he swiftly placed a hand on either side of her tense body, pinning her against the whitewashed wall. In the shadowy stable they might have been alone in the world. 'Shall we try a little experiment, then?'

No! her nerves screamed; already she was aware that she was trembling. She had been foolish, he could overwhelm her in seconds. They both knew it, even if she would never admit it.

'Please, Guy,' she whispered hoarsely, her eyes oddly pleading, 'you don't have to prove anything to me. If you'll just give me time, I'm sure I'll meet someone else and my emotions will develop naturally, then I'll be off your hands.'

'I don't have time . . .'

She blinked, unsure that she had heard properly, or, if she had, what to make of it. His harshly drawn breath, however, seemed to give her a brief advantage, which she pressed. 'I won't stay here any longer than I have to.'

'That isn't what we are trying to prove.' He actually smiled, if his lips did have a humourless twist as they descended on hers.

His body, smelling of sweat from a morning's hard work, crushed against Julia's as his powerful, sinewy arms left the wall and wrapped right round her. Their flesh, already warm, increased in heat until Julia felt she was burning. His mouth, hot and hungry, parted her unresisting lips and she was aware of a mocking satisfaction deep inside him. As she succumbed with a humiliating lack of fight to his probing mouth and exploring hands, she realised dimly he was proving his point, over and over again.

All her protests seemed lodged in her throat, sounding more like erotic whimpers. She felt his back bend as she tried to move away from him and he refused to allow it. The pounding of her heart drummed out all thought as his mouth manipulated hers expertly and cruelly, working its corrosive magic on her senses.

It was too much! Her mind was rapidly losing control as her body melted and pressed against him, as if determined to imprint itself for ever on every inch of his hard bone and muscle. A groan escaped her as her arms stole about his neck, and she hadn't the strength to fight their combined passion.

She knew instinctively that here in the darkness of the stables, he felt inclined to make her suffer more than a few kisses. She felt the hardness of his thighs telling her something she had never been conscious of before. When she stirred in silent protest, fighting more the rapturous betrayal of her own senses, Guy told her thickly to be quiet.

She couldn't believe, with his experience, he wasn't able to control the situation. 'Please . . .!' she murmured as his mouth moved over her skin with all the sensuous warmth of a caressing sun, 'Surely you've—you've had enough?'

'No.' His well-bred voice penetrated her shell-like

ears, scorning her halting attempt to restore them to
sanity. 'You owe me. You invade my house, my peace
of mind, break my property. Haven't you ever heard of
compensation?'

'Not this kind.'

'Can you think of a nicer way of repaying your debts.'

'Yes!' she returned fiercely.

He stared at her narrowly a long moment before
letting her go. 'At least you won't be so eager to argue
with me again,' he said mockingly.

Hating him, while not being able to pretend she
didn't understand him, Julia glared at him helplessly.
Fearing her shaking legs might give way under her, she
was forced to brace herself, her hands behind her on the
wall. From the way he was watching her, she was aware
that he knew this, and while it added to his satisfaction
he was only waiting until he was sure she had regained
her strength before leaving her.

'I'll see you at lunch,' he said at last, turning away.

Over lunch, which was always a family affair, to her
dismay, Julia found her eyes constantly dwelling on
him. As he talked to Lorraine and Mavis, much as she
tried to prevent it, her glance continually strayed in his
direction. He had showered and changed. Julia
wondered if he had been removing all traces of her
along with the sweat and dust. When he had poured her
wine she had smelled only after-shave and soap; a faint
if expensive torment for her delicate nostrils. As she had
lifted her glass to her lips, their eyes had caught and
held, and though she could read nothing from the total
darkness of his, she still shivered to think what her own
might have revealed.

Trying to fix her attention on the design of her plate
instead of his hard, handsome face, she was dimly
aware of the twins quarrelling. Something about a
catapult. Fortune, always the more forceful of the two,
was fiercely denying having broken it. Afterwards, Julia
realised this should have warned her if, as too often

happened these days, she hadn't been so absorbed in her own thoughts. As it was, she was aghast to hear Fitz insisting stubbornly:

'You did break it, just like you broke *Oncle* Guy's vase and blamed Julia!'

There was one of those brief, inexplicable silences which sometimes overtakes a group of people. Fitz's rather shrill treble voice must have reached everyone's ears quite clearly. Panic-striken, Julia exclaimed loudly, 'Fitz!' but it was too late.

She might have done better to have said nothing at all. As Guy's glance, accelerating with anger, sped from her flushed, unhappy face to Fortune's guilty one, she knew the game was up.

Lorraine, who had been forced to secretly ring Madame Boutin to get the full story of the broken vase, caught on immediately. Cleverly she had made much of Julia's fall from grace and had no wish to see her exonerated. 'I think we should let the matter rest, Guy darling,' she interposed sweetly, pretending concern for Fortune's sudden tears, 'We certainly don't wish to have the children upset, and who knows who was really to blame?'

'Please, Lorraine!' Guy shot her a glance that brought a sullen look to her face, an expression that boded ill for Julia.

Rising to his feet, he refused coffee. 'I'll see you in the office after you finish,' he spoke crisply to Julia. He didn't ask, he commanded, and she didn't dare disobey him. Refusing coffee too, she rushed upstairs to wash her perspiring hands and waited a few minutes until a feeling of sickness wore off before going back downstairs to join him.

'I want the truth!' he said grimly when at last she knocked on the office door and he bade her come in.

'First,' she fidgeted uncomfortably, playing for time, 'I—I'd like to thank you for not being angry with Fortune.'

'I am his uncle,' he reminded her curtly, his eyes expressionless on her white face, 'but because I didn't chastise him immediately that doesn't necessarily mean I won't. I'll admit I felt like putting him over my knee, there and then, but I managed to restrain myself. Once I hear the full story—the true one,' he emphasised curtly, 'I will be able to decide exactly what to say to him—and you.'

Didn't he ever lose control? Julia stared at him, shivering from the coldness of his voice which seemed to threaten her more than Fortune. Wouldn't it have been kinder to have smacked Fortune immediately and been done with it? The small boy was probably suffering now more than he would have done from a few light smacks on his bottom. Guy was so tall and dark, so very—she searched for the word—autocratic. Didn't he realise how easily he could strike fear into the hearts of weaker mortals with just one piercing glance from his hard eyes? She felt her own heart racing as he stared at her now, obviously waiting for her to say something.

With an effort she began to speak. 'Perhaps we should follow Lorraine's advice and forget about it?'

'Julia!'

'Oh, all right,' she swallowed, suddenly too weary to protest any further, 'if you insist.'

'I do,' he said impatiently, as she paused again. 'All this drama over one vase appears to be getting out of hand. I want an end to it.' As she still bit her lip uncertainly, he startled her by stepping nearer. Almost savagely he caught hold of her, running his hands up her bare arm. His grip on her shoulders was gentler and as he reached her nape he was almost caressing. When his hands came up to allow his fingers to explore her apprehensive face, Julia drew a sharp breath, realising his touch was persuasive but unable to find the willpower to object.

'Come on,' he murmured softly, 'spill the beans.'

It was such an English expression that it didn't help her composure. A sob escaped her, a hint of wild laughter, lending an incredible beauty to her storm-washed grey eyes. 'What is it you have to know,' she whispered unsteadily, 'that you don't know already? The boys ran into the *salon* and when I realised where they were—in your mother's special room—instead of ordering them out immediately, I began looking at a painting and forgot about them.'

Guy's dark brows met as she paused to gulp air. 'And when Fortune dropped the vase, you rushed over to him, while he ran away from it. You both reacted naturally, but it was wrong of you to let me believe you had broken it deliberately.'

'No,' she dared meet his blazing blue eyes, 'you thought that up yourself. Pierre and his mother thought I'd been careless, but you chose to think I'd done it on purpose, which was unforgivable of you!'

'Maybe,' he agreed shortly, his eyes still glittering, 'but you must agree that all the evidence was against you and it was a reasonable conclusion.'

'Unreasonable, I should say!'

Guy was unmoved. Like a lawyer, cross-examining, he coolly asked why.

'I was trying to protect Fortune!'

'No, you weren't,' he rasped, 'not really. You must have known very well that had you explained the situation, I might have chastised the boy, but it would have been over now and forgotten. No, I believe you're an opportunist, Julia. You saw a chance of getting rid of Pierre and grasped it. If you'd had any feeling for Pierre, you would have found a way to tell him what really happened.'

'Would he have believed me?'

'You could have given him the chance.'

'You must be joking, Guy! You were all so quick to think the worst of me, it was amazing!' Bitterly she added, 'I got so I didn't care . . .'

Moodily his eyes narrowed as he met her resentful ones. 'You're convinced that I've wronged you, but I'm not going to offer an apology. If you look into your heart you might discover you had other reasons than the one you were consciously aware of.'

Julia's lashes fell heavily on her cheeks and she wished she had been able to hide the guilty colour stealing under her skin. Why was Guy so often right, and so very confusing? 'I thought I was doing it for Fortune,' she whispered, feeling almost despicable.

'So you were—partly. But another time you should pause and examine your motives before you act so impulsively.'

'Yes.' She could only feel meek and rather bewildered. 'And Fortune?' she murmured.

'You mean what am I going to do about him? Nothing,' he replied calmly.

'You said you would smack him?'

'I said I felt like it.'

'But you won't.'

He smiled wryly, his hands leaving her shoulders, to where they had dropped after his exploration of her face. 'I should think that young man's thoughts have been more painful than anything I might administer physically. I imagine he's suffered enough. I might mention that deceiving others is frequently a waste of time as the truth usually comes out.'

'N-nothing more than that?' she stammered, astonished at such leniency from a not very tolerant man.

Guy sighed, as if at her lack of understanding. 'My nephew is not abnormally careless by nature and one can't reasonably expect his life to be totally free of accidents.'

Julia wished everything he said didn't fill her with increasing admiration. What a wonderful father he would make! She envied the woman who would bear his sons. He could make her sore and angry, but underneath, in the most secret parts of her, was always an emotion she hollowly suspected was love.

Forcing herself to speak lightly, she smiled at him. 'Once your sister is better, the twins will be happier. I'm sure of that.'

'And not so accident-prone. I agree.' The glance he bent on her eager face was intent and thoughtful, 'Fayme is much improved. In fact she is out of bed— Léon told me when I rang earlier. One of these days I must take you to meet her.'

Julia would have loved to have gone, but she didn't take Guy's suggestion too seriously. It had been more in the nature of a light remark; he hadn't promised. Most probably he would forget about it. He hadn't been to see Fayme for two weeks, and when he went again he would take Lorraine with him. He always did.

She was surprised, therefore, when Lorraine sought her out, one evening after dinner when Guy had retired to his study, and asked if she would like to go with him next day to visit his sister.

'Guy has to go on other business and Madame wants him to call and see Fayme. Madame wishes me to accompany him as she is old-fashioned enough to believe Fayme's delicate condition should only be discussed among women, but I'm rapidly becoming bored with the situation. Children,' she added with a disdainful shrug, 'I have always disliked, even to talk of them. I certainly shan't have any of my own.'

Julia didn't pretend to be startled by what she was hearing. It wasn't something she hadn't guessed all along. It did astonish her, though, that Lorraine should express such views out loud; she wondered if she did when Guy was around. And, if she was bored with going to Nice with Guy, why hadn't she said anything before?

'I enjoy going with him usually,' Lorraine said sharply, as if reading Julia's thoughts, 'but I feel I've a migraine coming on, that is why I'm asking you.'

Lorraine frequently had migraine when it suited her.

Julia frowned suspiciously. 'Guy may prefer to go by himself,' she demurred.

'You don't know much about Fayme's family, do you?' Lorraine countered.

Julia shook her head. 'I suppose not, but I have met her husband.'

'Did you know he's a famous director?'

'A film director?'

'Of course,' Lorraine replied coolly. 'You don't have to look so surprised. That's what he was doing in Germany, when Fayme became ill.'

'How—exciting,' Julia remarked, feeling such a remark was expected of her.

'Actually, I've been in one of his films,' Lorraine purred, not saying which one.

Julia was about to ask when she suddenly realised she knew nothing about French films, having had little opportunity to see any, even on television. 'How exciting,' she repeated, trying to look impressed. She was by Fayme's husband, but not Lorraine. However, she had no reason to doubt Lorraine's acting ability. Didn't she see evidence of it every day?

'Léon's always on the look-out for new talent.' Lorraine noted Julia's awed face with satisfaction. 'Actually,' she dropped her voice conspiringly, though they were alone in the room, 'when he was here he asked if you'd had any experience. He said you were beautiful, just what he was looking for.'

'Me?' Julia whispered incredulously. 'He never mentioned anything.'

'Circumstances weren't exactly favourable,' Lorraine reminded her. 'I advised him to wait. Guy doesn't know, but he approached me about you again, the last time I was in Nice.'

Julia glanced at her uneasily. 'I'm flattered, of course, but—well, I don't know the first thing about acting.'

'Few do, to begin with,' Lorraine shrugged, 'but there

are those who have made enough from their first film to keep them in comfort for months.'

'That might be possible for some people,' Julia agreed doubtfully, 'but it must be the exception rather than the rule, and I've never seen myself as an actress.'

'It could help you to be independent,' Lorraine pointed out sweetly, 'I don't suppose you want to rely on Guy's charity for the rest of your life. If Léon took you on you would be free to do as you liked.'

'Did Guy ask you to tell me this?' Julia felt herself growing suddenly cold.

'No,' Lorraine replied so hastily that Julia believed her, but just as she became aware of enormous relief, Lorraine went on, 'He might not approve, so I'd say nothing to him, if I were you, until you've seen Léon. If you had a job to go to, I'm sure he wouldn't try and keep you here. You can take it from me, he'd be delighted!'

CHAPTER SIX

ALL the way to Nice, which was quite a distance from Arles, the nearest town to where Guy lived, Julia puzzled over what Lorraine had told her. She was conscious that Guy found her abstracted, and in a way when her thoughts wandered she felt ashamed, for she realised it was very kind of him to take her with him to see Fayme.

It was the uncertainty of the situation that bothered her. Neither Guy nor Mavis had mentioned anything about Léon's occupation and she didn't want to tell him what Lorraine had said for fear he would think they had been gossiping behind his back. She could always have pretended to have overheard the twins talking about their father but if it wasn't true that he was a film director, she was going to look very foolish! Why she should imagine Lorraine had been deceiving her, Julia didn't know. She always had the feeling that Lorraine couldn't be completely trusted.

'Why so silent?' Guy queried, slanting her a brow-raised glance.

'I'm sorry,' she flushed slightly, without meeting his eyes, 'I was just looking at the scenery.'

His mouth quirked as he appeared to believe her. 'As it's supposed to be one of the most famous stretches of coast in the world, I may perhaps forgive you.'

'Forgive—me?'

'That your attention has strayed,' he replied dryly.

This time she did glance at him, but the mockery she encountered made her look away quickly. Uncomfortably she wished he didn't so easily see through her and that the directness of his brilliant blue eyes didn't make her heart race as if it was competing

96

with the car. Her voice seemed thin in her ears as she said hastily, 'This is the Côte d'Azur?'

'Yes. It stretches from Marseilles to Menton. Unfortunately, famous though it might be, in places it isn't so lovely any more.' He gestured briefly towards some distant housing developements and skyscrapers which Julia took for hotels. 'Cement can ruin anything.'

Julia didn't feel qualified to agree. The beauty of this rugged coast with its innumerable creeks, deserted little beaches, bright blue sea and spectacular views struck her as being impressive. There no doubt were areas such as Guy had noted disparagingly, but on the whole it still seemed to have a lot going for it.

'Does your sister actually live in Nice?' she asked, her thoughts returning again to Fayme and her family, hoping that if she mentioned them, Guy would be more willing to talk about them than he had been in the past.

'Not right in the town itself,' he rejoined. 'They have a villa near Juan-les-Pins, which is really a suburb of Antibes.'

'I hadn't heard of it.'

His foot must have pressed harder on the accelerator, because the powerful Ferrari leapt forward. 'It's better known for its night life,' he said curtly.

'And Nice?'

'Big and sprawling, the undisputed capital of the Riviera. It seems to have everything, depending on what you like. It has a lot of big city attractions such as numerous movie houses and concerts.'

'Sounds exciting,' she remarked, without adding that, as Guy described it, it didn't appeal to her.

'If excitement is what you're after.'

About to say it wasn't, Julia paused. If Fayme's husband was in films and if by some incredible chance he did offer her a job and she felt compelled to take it, Guy might never be willing to let her go if she confessed beforehand how even the thought of such smart places and people almost frightened her.

'I suppose a little does no harm,' she answered feebly.

'Does that mean you find living in the Camargue dull?' he enquired shortly.

'Only sometimes,' she forced herself to reply, wondering how he would react if she were to say that she loved his home and would never find it dull. And that she was almost sure she loved him.

After this he appeared to concentrate on his driving and the sudden grimness of his profile, combined with her soul-shaking discovery, kept her silent again. This time, though, he didn't try to break it.

The villa where his sister and brother-in-law lived was large and modern, such a contrast to Champonale, Guy's estate in the Camargue, that Julia gasped.

'Impressed, are you?' Guy's voice was coldly sarcastic as they came to a halt on the broad, gravelled drive and his head swung to catch her startled expression.

'Who wouldn't be?' Julia clung stubbornly to her chosen role, feeling something of an actress already.

'Big isn't necessarily beautiful,' he retorted curtly, 'nor is everything that glitters gold. It might pay you to remember, Julia.'

She didn't understand his mood and didn't try and discover what lay behind it. He had been amiable enough when they had set out and she couldn't decide what had angered him. Defensively she avoided the harshness of his face, letting her glance wander in the direction of the voices she could hear in the distance. Through a screen of trees she caught a glimpse of blue water, which she guessed was a pool. As Fayme was ill, she was surprised that there were people here, obviously enjoying themselves.

'Shall we go inside?' Guy grasped her arm, looking disapproving rather than surprised, 'I'd like to know what's going on.'

His sister, who Julia knew he expected to find in bed, was sitting in the lounge when they were ushered into the room by a well trained manservant. The only concession Fayme made to being ill was that she had her feet up. Otherwise, apart from a slight pallor, she looked remarkably well—nothing like the invalid Julia had anticipated.

'Guy!' The pleasure in Fayme's eyes as well as her voice revealed she was pleased to see him. 'How wonderful!'

'You're up?' As his glance rested on the other girl, Julia recognised his silky tones apprehensively. 'I thought you were supposed to be in bed?'

Fayme didn't shrink, as Julia was sure she would have done if Guy had spoken to her in a similar manner. She replied with a bright smile, clearly used to appeasing him. 'My doctor said I might get up three days ago. He is so pleased with me, he has promised, if I behave myself, I may have the twins home in a week or two.'

'If you behave yourself!' Guy repeated, the dryness of his voice seeming to suggest she didn't know how to. 'Why didn't you let us know?' he asked more curtly. 'Mavis would have been relieved.'

'I wanted to!' Fayme's smooth young face, bearing little resemblance to her brother's, was indignant. 'As soon as Doctor Lanson told me I was improving, I thought of Maman straight away, but Léon advised me to wait until we were sure. I intended giving her a ring in the morning.'

Guy sighed, then introduced Julia, as if he had only just remembered she was there.

'Why, *bonjour*, cousin from England!' Fayme exclaimed warmly in French, and, because Fayme seemed so delighted to see her, Julia replied involuntarily in the same language.

'Oh, *formidable*!' Fayme clapped her hands together with a teasing laugh. 'I believed for a moment you were another of Guy's beautiful girl-friends. This is a pleasant surprise.'

Guy ignored her remark without a flicker of an

eyelid. 'I was going to leave Julia with you, as I have an engagement and I thought it would be a chance for you to get acquainted with each other.'

'But of course you can leave Julia with me,' Fayme broke in. 'What makes you think you can't?'

'You have other visitors,' he glanced in the direction of the gardens.

'Other visitors? Oh,' she waved a careless hand, 'It is only Léon auditioning a few hopeful souls for his latest film. Actually I think the cast is chosen, but there are a few things to iron out. He just thought, as I am so much better, he would do it at home. Since I've been ill,' she added complacently, 'he doesn't care to be far away from me.'

Guy frowned. 'They won't be coming in here?'

'No!' Fayme pulled a charming face at him. 'I gather it's Julia you're worried about, but you can rest assured she won't come to any harm. Léon is not without a conscience, you know. He has a proper regard for his wife's health and he doesn't throw little lambs to the wolves.'

Julia noticed Fayme's lips quirk mockingly as Guy turned to leave, then she saw her amused expression change thoughtfully as he snapped grimly over his shoulder, 'He'd better not, or he'll rue the day.'

'Now I wonder,' Fay said slowly, as he nodded to Julia and the door closed behind him, 'what's got into him?'

Oddly enough, Julia didn't feel like cashing in on the note of curiosity in Fayme's voice. Her own conclusions, that Guy didn't want her led astray until he had her respectably married off, might only give Fayme cause for further amusement.

'I think he works too hard,' she answered, as Fayme glanced at her enquiringly.

'You're probably right,' Fayme agreed, relaxing lazily on her pile of cushions again. 'You know,' she smiled at Julia wryly, 'before I married Léon, I led a very sheltered life and Guy still thinks he can dictate to me.'

Julia was surprised to find herself resenting the note of criticism in her cousin's voice. 'He does think a lot of you,' she said quickly.

'I know,' Fayme smiled mischievously but not maliciously. 'He has strong family feelings. It's something I'm used to and he seems to have developed the same protective instincts towards you.'

Julia realised the truth of this, even though she knew he would be pleased to get rid of her. 'He feels responsible, I think, although he doesn't need to.'

'He's fairly typical of a lot of Frenchmen, you'll find,' Fayme warned. 'Times are changing, but, especially in rural areas, old conventional customs die hard. The average Frenchman still likes to guide and rule his family, but young people do have much more freedom today, even if they have to fight for it.'

'Yes,' Julia agreed, but before she could add any more, Fayme was apologising hastily for being remiss and asking her to sit down. Then she rang for coffee and while they drank it they talked together, discovering an immediate liking for each other. Fayme dwelt lightly on the problems that were making her pregnancy difficult, but seemed more eager to talk of the twins, whom she was clearly missing a lot. Julia was happy to provide a first-hand account of them, omitting to mention the broken vase, but touching amusingly on the lesser pranks they got up to, making their mother laugh. By the time she finished, she was pleased to see Fayme looking so much happier.

'Lorraine has never been able to tell me much,' Fayme complained.

'Perhaps,' Julia said carefully, 'because your brother demands a lot of her time.'

'Perhaps,' Fayme retorted waspishly, 'it's the other way round. Lorraine has always fancied Guy, but, for him, I think the spark is missing.'

'The – spark?'

'Hmm.' Fayme watched Julia closely, 'No, perhaps you are still too innocent? When I met Léon I felt it straight away, like a flame. It's still there, but it's not easy to explain.'

No, it wasn't. Julia's silent agreement caused her to flush, making Fayme's eyes narrow again thoughtfully. She seemed about to say something, but changed her mind as her husband entered the room through the open French window, obviously, by the anxious expression on his face, to check on his wife.

'Are you all right, *ma bien-aimée*?' he enquired, a moment before his sharp glance fell on the girl by his wife's side. 'Julia!' he sounded surprised but pleased. 'This is good. Did you come with Lorraine?'

'She came with Guy.'

'Guy!' his brows rose as he glanced quickly at his wife before returning his attention to Julia. 'Don't tell me, my dear brother-in-law has brought you here and gone off and left you?'

Guy's remark about wolves returned, but Julia could see nothing of the wolf in Léon's genial face. He looked quite different today from the rather staid business man she had taken him for when he had come to Champonale to tell them of Fayme's illness. In a pair of jeans and a tee-shirt, he seemed somehow years younger.

When Lorraine had mentioned that he would like her in one of his films, Julia hadn't taken her very seriously, but in the next half hour, as Léon, as if taking advantage of Guy's absence, deserted his guests to put such a proposition to her, she was forced to believe Lorraine hadn't been merely teasing her.

'I wish to do this film in about two months,' he explained, 'and I'm searching for a girl exactly like you—young, beautiful and virginal.'

Such frankness brought a flush to Julia's cheeks as she stammered, 'But I've had no experience, *monsieur*!'

'Léon,' he said, then, dryly, 'That is what I want, a girl without experience. It isn't a big part, but it is important. If I thought you couldn't handle it, I wouldn't have suggested it.'

'I'm tempted,' she confessed, without stating reasons.

'I shouldn't hesitate, if I were you,' Fayme encouraged, too sure of Léon's adoration and with too much respect for his career to be jealous. 'You would live with us, of course, and I know the twins would love to have you. It would help enormously if you were here to take them off my hands occasionally and you would still have lots of time to get some proper coaching.'

Julia tried to feel enthusiastic about becoming an actress. 'What if I fail?'

Fayme said quickly, before Léon could intervene, 'I can't see that happening, but if it did, I'm sure Léon would find a niche for you somewhere. Or you could always stay and help with the new baby. We have a full-time staff, but no nursemaid.'

Feeling overwhelmed by such trusting friendliness, Julia had to accept. Léon's reassurance that she would be an immediate success didn't make her feel so happy as the genuine rapport between Fayme and herself. It seemed an added bonus that her cousin liked her and Julia knew she could trust her.

Brief details were discussed—the terms Léon quoted she considered too generous until he reminded her wryly that even the top stars sometimes had periods without work, and it was agreed that she should come to them at the end of the week. They hadn't, unfortunately, allowed for Guy's furious disapproval!

Fayme had let drop that he was visiting a retired professor, one of his tutors who had taught him at university. He was late getting back and was persuaded to stay to dinner. As they drank their aperitifs, before moving into the dining-room, Julia wondered if this wouldn't be a good moment to break the news that from the weekend she would be working for Léon. Guy had brought her a glass of St Raphael, one of the sweet French aperitifs which she had discovered was more popular than sherry in France, and he appeared to have forgotten he still had his hand on her arm. They were both casually dressed. Julia had on a cotton skirt and sleeveless top, and she was confused that the coolness of his fingers should strike such heat through her veins. She began to tremble and knew he was aware of her reaction as his grip tightened. In desperation, she almost revealed how relieved she would be to escape him, when she suddenly noticed the slight, warning shake of Fayme's head.

Guy's possessive attitude was clearly making Fayme cautious as well as curious, but Julia felt grateful when she wandered over to where they were standing and began asking Guy how he had found his professor.

While they talked, because she didn't know the professor so couldn't take part in their conversation, Julia stared blindly through the window. The gardens were quiet, the crowd round the pool long ago dispersed. Julia, in the course of the afternoon, had met some of them including a cousin of Léon's who had had to leave early, though not for the same reason as the others. André Tissier wasn't in films, though he obviously enjoyed what he called hobnobbing with the stars. His father owned a vineyard some distance from the Camargue and André was in charge as his parents were away from home. Julia might have felt flattered, but she wasn't, that André had been immediately attracted by her fairness and promised her would soon be in touch.

There had been one woman who had begged to be allowed to stay and see Guy, announcing plaintively that she had dined with him several weeks ago and never seen him since. Julia tried to forget how voluptuous Chloe, as Léon called her, had been. She also tried to stop wondering if Guy was in love with her. She had felt ashamed at how relieved she had been when Léon told Chloe firmly to disappear as Guy and he had business to discuss.

After dinner, a meal both beautifully cooked and served but which tasted curiously like sawdust to Julia, Fayme tactfully broached the subject of her new employment. Fayme was allowed to stay up for dinner but had still to go to bed early. Julia suspected, with a sudden rush of apprehension, that she had left it until the last moment so she could, if necessary, beat a hasty retreat.

'Julia is keen to find something to do, Guy,' Fayme began, after gaining his attention. As he had been staring at Julia narrow-eyed, as if sensing something was disturbing her, it must have seemed a good opportunity.

'Is she?' His voice was quite without interest, and because his eyes remained on her face, Julia realised her guilty flush must be quite obvious to him.

'You—you know I am.' Conscious of how her voice faltered, she grabbed her half-finished Burgundy, then put it down again just as quickly. No sense in choking, which she seemed in danger of doing without any help! She had already, she suspected, drunk too much, and during the next few minutes, the voice of instinct warned her, the thing she would need most was a clear head!

Guy's mouth curled in an attitude obviously disparaging. 'I have heard you mention it occasionally, but I believe you're already familiar with my views on the subject.'

This, judging from his tone, his grim demeanour, was the end of it. If pressed, he would refuse to discuss it. Julia gazed at him, until it clearly became a battle of wills between them, then she lowered her head, abysmally defeated. Fayme, however, persevered.

'Léon has offered her a part in one of his films.'

Léon took over as if on cue. 'It's on the level, Guy. She will stay with us and we will look after her.'

'I'm sure!' Getting to his feet, Guy spoke icily. 'Come, Julia, it's time we were going.'

He refused to even talk about it! 'But—Oh, please!' Julia begged, suddenly angry. 'You have to wait . . . Let Léon explain . . .!'

'Do you think I need to?' he rasped, so tall and autocratic he subdued them all immediately with one glance from glittering blue eyes. Speaking to Julia, his voice was like flint. 'I have no doubt that the offer is genuine, but it is not for you. I'm familiar enough with life on the set to know what it can do to a *jeune fille*. And Léon couldn't be with you all the time.'

'She has to grow up sometime, Guy!' Léon protested, gesticulating wildly behind them as Guy dragged Julia out to the car. 'She's old enough anyway.'

'You mean—to be seduced by one of your team?'

'*Tiens*—your opinion of me!' Léon raged.

'Not of you personally, although your motives are questionable. Guy opened the car and while practically flinging Julia into it, glanced at his brother-in-law cynically. 'Let's say I appreciate how you keep my sister in comparative luxury, but not always the way you do it.'

With a roar they shot down the drive while Julia was still trying to find her breath. Resentment boiled up within her until she could scarcely contain it. She had scarcely been allowed a word in her own defence! Guy looked so thunderous he almost frightened her to death, but for her own sake she had to make a stand. If she allowed him to trample over her, he would use the same tactics again in the future.

And, she argued with herself feverishly, she had to get away from him, for reasons she couldn't explain. Briefly she was moved to hollow, silent laughter. Ironically he might be quite willing to let her go if she had the courage to confess she was falling in love with him.

Swallowing hard, she reminded herself that the

English had frequently fought the French and won, if sometimes it had been a matter of opinion. 'Don't you think you were terribly rude back there?' she ventured. 'Léon and Fayme are very nice people. I'm sure they didn't deserve having you lose your temper with them, the way you did.'

It was a mild enough approach but she was gathering her strength for a more direct attack. Apparently, though, no one had ever dared criticise Guy Guerard before. If possible, he looked even more furious.

'I should never have brought you here,' he snapped, harshly. 'It's my own fault, but I won't allow you to question what I say—to anyone!'

'Please, Guy . . .' the anger faded from her voice with an alarming lack of consistency, which didn't appear to mollify him in the least.

'Be quiet, will you!' he increased his speed until they seemed to be hurtling into the encroaching darkness. 'I'll find a place to park shortly. We'll talk then.'

It must be a threat. He certainly wouldn't be stopping to apologise! Julia shivered as he took a diversion, skidding on to a lonely, deserted road. 'Why here?' she whispered, as he braked in the middle of it, 'What if someone wants to get past?'

'They won't,' he replied indifferently. 'I had some property in this area once. This road only leads to some marshy land.'

'Couldn't this wait until when we get home?' she asked, gazing around her apprehensively. Her nerves were strung taut, but it wasn't the darkness she was afraid of.

'No!' he was wholly adamant, not giving an inch. 'If we have to talk this thing out, we'll do it where there's no risk of Mavis hearing and being upset. She will probably have gone to bed by the time we return, but I'm taking no risks. And you have a habit of retreating to your bedroom when something doesn't agree with you, and I have no intention of seeking you out there.'

As though she encouraged him to! And the phrases he used—'doesn't agree with you'—as if she were a spoilt child!

'I think you're despicable!' she blazed.

'Enough!' he retorted as she persisted.

'You have no right to interfere in my affairs,' she muttered stubbornly.

'I have every right.'

'Not to stop me choosing what I want to do!'

'Was that really what you wanted to do?' he challenged coldly. 'Become a cheap little star overnight?'

'That's not fair!' she cried, unwilling to answer directly. 'Acting's an honourable profession. Plenty of people succeed in it.'

'Usually after spending years at drama school and practically dying of starvation in minor parts. Or did you forget the hard work in anticipation of the excitement?'

How horrible he could be! Julia lifted her chin, her grey eyes stormy. 'What excitement?'

'Being held in some stage hero's arms, of course. Didn't you ever pause to think you didn't need to go to such lengths to find a few kisses?'

Her temper flared in the face of such mockery. 'I'm not interested in such things!'

'Aren't you?' She might have guessed what was. coming next as his arms reached for her in the dim light, but, as always, she was unprepared when he took hold of her. 'I can give you kisses and excitement, any man could, if that's what it takes to satisfy you,' Guy muttered insultingly.

'Stop it!' she cried, her voice lower than she would have liked as she tried to struggle against him. He was not to be so easily got rid of, however. The next instant his arms were sliding round her shoulders and his lips were on hers. He began kissing her brutally, demolishing rather than dissolving her resistance, as he had done on other occasions. She wanted to resist, but she couldn't. Guy held her so tightly she couldn't so much as move. Yet, as the pressure of his mouth increased and her head was thrown back, she felt a powerful wave of desire surging right through her.

'Please, Guy,' she pleaded, when the pressure of his mouth eased, 'why are you doing this?'

'To supply you with excitement, of course.' He loosened his grip on her waist to clasp her face in his hand, his eyes, hard and mocking, impaling hers. 'You were feeling in need of some, even on our way to Nice. I distinctly recall you saying so, so you can't complain.'

'What makes you think I find kissing you exciting?' she retorted rashly, desperately trying to give the impression that she hated it, in the hope that he would let her go. 'It doesn't make me feel a thing!'

'Doesn't it?' The mockery in his glance increased. 'Perhaps I haven't tried hard enough?'

As his mouth descended again, Julia attempted to twist away, but no matter how hard she tried, he held her with contemptuous ease, leaning over her, pressing her to the whole length of his virile body. Again she fought against a response, but her physical strength and emotional endurance were puny compared to his determination. She could feel the pulse beating wildly in her throat and, as his fingers touched it, she knew he could easily discover for himself how deeply he affected her. He must know she was totally helpless against the persuasion of his hands and her own rapidly heightening senses.

His lips turned the blood in her veins to liquid fire as they crushed and probed, then miraculously softened. She was so unprepared for the gentleness that replaced his harsh passion that briefly she stiffened, expecting to be subjected to another form of punishment. But there was nothing frightening in the way he unbuttoned her thin cotton blouse. His hands were like a whisper, she might have been more aware of a soft breeze on her skin. It wasn't until she felt them on her breasts, lightly and sensuously stroking, that she became conscious of his deviousness. He no longer needed to hold her in a vice-like grip. His every movement was sending flames roaring through her, mopping up every pocket of resistance.

There was no room for escape. At first she had intended to, but his overpowering attraction swiftly undermined any such intention. As he continued to caress her and his mouth wandered insidiously over her heated skin, she gave in.

With a muffled cry, her arms crept round his neck and when he groaned thickly at such evidence of surrender, and his lips returned to hers, she opened her mouth to him, letting him explore its melting sweetness until the strength drained from her very bones. His hands clenched hard on the flesh of her back, as though he were trying to keep them there, but, as her response increased, they moved to cup the fullness of her breasts, his fingers massaging her hardening nipples. Long before he stopped, her body was crying out for something she didn't understand.

'Guy?' she whispered as he slowly withdrew. 'Is there something wrong?'

His face, she noticed, had gone strangely white. 'You haven't done anything wrong, Julia, but maybe I have.'

'You mean—because you consider I'm a child?'

He still loomed over her, as though he had forgotten where he was, but while his blue eyes burned over her, he made no attempt to touch her. 'I haven't considered you a child for a long time.'

Why did the admission seem torn from him? Julia's tormented eyes asked questions she dared not put in to words, but his expression told her plainly that he was in no mood for explanations.

He did elaborate a little, however, perhaps taking pity on her as her fumbling fingers, rebuttoning her blouse, must have revealed something of her inner agitation. 'You aren't a child any more, Julia, but you're a young woman without experience. That you're so young and beautiful makes you very vulnerable.'

'Please,' she gasped fiercely, her temper suddenly rising, 'don't start lecturing me about having to grow up!' Her eyes flashed. 'Plenty of girls my age are married and have families.'

'Mon Dieu!' his voice was suddenly grim. 'You talk of babies when you've never even been in a man's bed!'

'So you think I'm a late developer?' she stared at him with a belligerence she couldn't seem to control. If she couldn't love him why did she have this terrible urge to fight him?

He refused to be drawn, although he did advise her to calm down. He appeared to feel he had a duty to soothe her, in acknowledging he was responsible for the deep turmoil let loose inside her. His glance was wary on the bright colour fluctuating too rapidly in the paleness of her cheeks, the stormy greyness of her eyes dilating feverishly. 'If you are a late developer,' he said more gently, 'perhaps it's because of the way you've been brought up.'

'Yes . . .?' she clutched at this like a drowning man might clutch at a straw. She had been properly brought up. How could emotions, even out-of-control ones, change one's basic character? 'I've always been very conventional,' she said stiffly.

'But pretty wild underneath.'

Did she detect a glitter of laughter in his eyes? 'You have no grounds. . . .'

'Apart from experiencing it personally.'

Now his mouth was quirking so unashamedly that she was surprised she didn't feel like hitting him. Realising he was trying, for her sake, to lighten the atmosphere between them stayed the hand she had been about to raise. Instead she found herself more than willing to meet him halfway.

'I—I'm sorry I lost my temper,' she tried bravely to

look straight at him. 'I'm sorry, too, that I accepted an offer of work without first consulting you.'

Guy eyed her thoughtfully. 'I'd like to believe you really mean that, Julia. I don't want you feeling resentful.'

She smiled wryly through the darkness. 'Somehow I don't think I'm cut out to be a film star, but,' she added, without intending to, 'Your sister did say I could help to look after the twins and the new baby when it arrives.'

'Time to consider this later,' he replied coolly. 'Meanwhile, I don't intend exposing you to Léon's powers of persuasion.'

'I'm sure he doesn't mean any harm,' she said quickly, 'and I do like Fayme.'

'I could see it was mutual. Had you any idea Léon was going to offer you a part?' he asked, with deceptive lightness.

'Lorraine said . . .'

As Julia paused abruptly on an impatient gasp, Guy exclaimed without surprise, 'I thought as much.'

Julia felt forced to speak up in Lorraine's defence as she had so foolishly betrayed her. 'You mustn't blame anyone. Lorraine guessed I was looking for work and was only trying to help.'

Holding up a hand, Guy snapped, 'Please spare me!'

'Well, after all,' Julia stammered, hating to make trouble. 'You can't blame her for wanting you to herself. Once you're married I'll have to look for somewhere else to live, and it would be easier if I could find a good job.'

He sighed and started the car, reversing from the lane on to the highway again. 'If you still feel the same way in six months' time,' he said curtly, 'we will talk about some training for a proper job. Until then I'm afraid you must content yourself with Champonale.'

It was late when they arrived home and everyone was in bed. Even Lorraine had retired, which made Julia wonder, as she usually stayed up until after midnight.

Guy glanced at her wan face with observant eyes. 'I'd go to bed as well, if I were you. Unless you'd like some coffee? It must be my fault you missed it after dinner.'

Julia thanked him but refused, although she would have loved to have shared a midnight rendezvous in the big, shadowy kitchen with him. 'I'd better not,' she smiled ruefully. 'It will do me more good to have a wash. I must look a mess.'

'Are you fishing for compliments?' Guy placed a caressing hand on her gleaming head, while regarding her with a glint of mockery. 'You must know you always look beautiful.'

She drew back sharply, not trusting herself so near him—aware of what even the touch of his hand could do to her. 'Goodnight, Guy.'

As she turned from him, she was surprised when his arm shot out to pull her back. 'I forgot to ask,' he explained his action suavely, 'who else did you meet at Fayme's?'

She stared at his broad, deep chest, though it didn't do much for her composure. Drawing a trembling breath, she uttered the name of the woman who had been painfully at the back of her mind all evening. 'Someone called Chloe, among others. She was anxious to see you again.'

CHAPTER SEVEN

'CHLOE Hervé?'

'Yes,' Julia had forgotten the woman's surname. Now she remembered it clearly and despised herself for asking, 'Is she a special friend?'

'No.'

Relief warred with doubt as she raised her eyes, searching his face. 'She said she had dined with you.'

'Among others. It was a party to do with a film première, if I remember correctly. One of Léon's more spectacular successes, which Fayme begged me to attend. Chloe Hervé had a leading role and I admired her performance, but that was all.'

Julia didn't try and hide a sigh of relief, and for the first time since arriving home, she felt sure she would sleep. Noting Guy's faint amusement, she flushed, exclaiming hastily, 'I was thinking of Lorraine.'

His amusement faded and he retorted curtly. 'Why think of either of them? *Bonne nuit,* Julia.'

Next morning he woke her up while the rest of the household was still sleeping. Threading his hands through thick, shining strands of fair hair, he found her bare shoulders under the covers and turned her over. *'Bonjour,'* he murmured, as she opened dazed, uncomprehending eyes, 'Do you always sleep with so little on?'

Suddenly realising where she was and who was with her and what he was doing, Julia gazed up at him, mutely protesting. Instead of meeting her indignant eyes, he avoided them, viewing the nervous pulse in her throat ironically.

'What do you want?' she whispered, suddenly wishing only that it was her.

'Many things,' he teased, 'all of which I hope to acquire with patience. A friendly kiss wouldn't come amiss, for a start.'

'Guy!' she gulped, conscious that her hot cheeks might be encouraging him. 'Do be serious!'

'I am,' he sighed, turning away, his dark face suddenly brooding. 'Stay under your sheet, my little puritan, I didn't come to harm you.'

'I don't suppose you did,' she said, and waited.

'It was merely something I forgot, last night.' He stopped by the window. She had thrown it wide the evening before and he leaned out. She heard him take a deep breath of the pure morning air as though he needed it. 'I think it would be wiser not to mention Léon's offer of employment to Mavis. She wouldn't approve, and you would only receive another lecture.'

Was he trying to apologise—if in a roundabout way? Gazing longingly at his broad back, noting the muscles rippling across his broad shoulders, she decided not to tempt fate by asking. 'Won't Fayme tell her?' she asked instead.

'No, I intend giving her a ring before breakfast. That's what I came to see you about. I'm going straight out and I didn't want to miss you.'

'You'd better warn Fayme not to mention it to—to anyone else, either,' she stammered, having almost referred to Lorraine.

'Don't worry,' said Guy darkly, recrossing her room, pausing with his hand on the door. 'Leave it to me.'

If only she could! Despondently she jumped straight out of bed, after he had gone, and rushed to the bathroom to take a shower. She would love to leave everything to him, let him make all the final decisions. If she ever married, she would want a husband who would let her take an intelligent interest in his business. But, in an old-fashioned way, she supposed, she would like him to be strong enough to lean on. As she dried herself she sighed, conscious that she was day dreaming in vain. Guy was already spoken for, so it was obvious that her hopes could come to nothing. She must manage on her own, or at least learn not to rely on the help of a man in love with another woman.

When she went down for breakfast, Guy was gone. Hortense, bringing her coffee, reminded her that he had a lot to do when she asked where he was.

'He breeds bulls and horses, and they are all to raise and manage.' She folded her arms across her ample bosom while Julia drank her cup of hot coffee. 'He has also an estate farther up the Rhone, several miles east of Montélimar.'

Julia nodded. 'I haven't seen a bullfight yet,' she smiled at Hortense wryly. 'I'm not sure that I want to.'

Hortense shrugged. 'If you remain here you will eventually. They have them all the time in Arles, in the huge Roman amphitheatre which holds twenty-five thousand. Every Sunday in summer they take place. It is an impressive sight, *mademoiselle*.'

'I can imagine!'

'You must get Monsieur Guy to take you one day,' the housekeeper went on in rapid French.

'He goes?' Julia was learning to follow like a native.

'*Oui*. Once he was a brilliant *razateur*.'

'A—a bullfighter?'

'Don't look so alarmed, *mademoiselle*,' Hortense's black eyes sparkled with amusement. 'It was long ago, when he was your age perhaps, certainly not much older. He was quite famous, but I think he did it for the money.'

'The money?'

'His father was inclined to be tight-fisted.'

Julia gulped, feeling suddenly very cold despite the warmth of the morning. 'But wasn't it dangerous?'

'The *course à la cocarde* isn't the bullfight where the bull is killed,' Hortense explained kindly after taking a shrewd glance at Mademoiselle's pale and betraying face. 'The bullfighter only has to pick the cockade from between the horns of the animal as it charges.'

'And Guy did that?'

'Do not fret, *mademoiselle*. He always got out of the way in time and he only did it for a year or two.'

'So he doesn't do it now.' Julia couldn't hide her relief.

'No. In a few years' time he will be forty. Even so,' Hortense declared, with visible pride, 'if he wished to it would not be beyond him. He is a man, that one!'

Trying to stop trembling at the thought of Guy being in such danger, for all Hortense obviously attempted to treat the matter lightly, Julia was forced to wait until the strength returned to her legs before she was able to run upstairs and speak to Mavis.

Guy had already told Hortense how Fayme was keeping better, and apparently he had been to see his stepmother as well. He appeared to have had quite a busy morning before he's even set foot outside! Julia thought waspishly, trying to hide her love and the fear she felt for him, even from herself.

Mavis, who rarely rose before mid-morning, was used to her family trooping in and out of her bedroom and she was pleased to see Julia.

'Guy came early,' she confessed. 'He knew I'd be waiting for news of Fayme. You don't know what a relief it is to know she's almost recovered at last.'

Julia felt ashamed. She had resented Guy stealing the limelight, so full had she been of her own importance, yet, she suspected, he hadn't waited until after he'd had breakfast, as she had done, before coming to relieve Mavis's anxious mind!

'I'm delighted,' Mavis sighed rather tremulously as Julia sat down on the chair which was always beside the bed. 'I'll miss the twins, of course, when they go, but I mustn't be selfish.'

'I imagine Fayme brings them to see you often,' Julia smiled.

'Not as often as I would like.' Mavis's brows knitted in a flickering frown. 'Fayme and Léon lead a busy life, as I gather you've discovered?'

Julia nodded but made no other comment. She was tempted to, as she was curious about what seemed to have been a conspiracy of silence between Guy and her aunt regarding Léon's occupation, but remembering Guy's caution, she restrained herself. At this stage, anyway, she had no wish to encourage the embarrassing questions which Aunt Mavis might easily ask if she knew exactly what had happened yesterday.

She heard Mavis murmuring abstractedly, 'I could go and visit them, I suppose. They ask me often enough. You could come as well. Guy tells me Fayme likes you.'

'Yes——' Julia hesitated on a shock of dismay. She didn't think Guy would be willing to let her go back to Nice in a hurry, even with Mavis. Then she decided it was no use worrying over something which might never happen. Her aunt was always planning various trips, but during all the weeks Julia had lived at Champonale, she couldn't remember her ever actually going anywhere.

She was grateful when the twins came running in, saving her an evasive reply, and a few minutes later, as she saw how their constant high spirits exhausted their adoring but frail *grand'mère*, she took them away.

'I'll see you at lunch.' Mavis gave Julia such a grateful and affectionate glance as she ushered the boys outside that a lump came to Julia's throat. Her aunt was a darling. If she gained nothing else from her stay in France, she would always be richer from knowing her.

The twins were in a restless mood. They wanted to ride out to the *étangs* and Julia, because she was feeling restless too, agreed to take them. She still wasn't very good on a horse, certainly not in the same class as Lorraine, but she liked riding and hoped to improve with practice.

To her surprise, Lorraine joined them at the stables, extremely smart in well tailored jodhpurs, as opposed to Julia's jeans. Ruefully Julia glanced down at them. She had three pairs now, thanks to Guy's generosity, but she realised they didn't compare with a proper riding outfit.

Lorraine, she knew, wasn't keen on exercise unless there was some purpose behind it, and as, at Champonale, it was usually Guy and he was nowhere to be seen, Julia was curious. She had little doubt, though, that she would soon discover what it was all about.

She didn't have long to wait. Breaking through an excited exchange between Fortune and Fitz on the best way of finding some wild horses, Lorraine turned to her sharply.

'Well,' she exclaimed, 'how did you get on?'

Julia sighed at her own lack of foresight. She might have guessed! 'Fine, thank you,' she replied politely, deliberately evasive.

Lorraine's eyes cooled impatiently. 'You know what I mean! Did Léon not offer you work?'

'Yes,' Julia pinned an indifferent smile on her face, 'but I refused.'

'Refused?' Lorraine sounded outraged. 'Why, in heaven's name, should you refuse?'

Julia feared the other girl thought she had taken leave of her senses, but although it was Lorraine who had first told her about Léon, Julia considered what had happened at Nice wasn't really any of her business. 'I didn't feel I was up to it,' she shrugged casually.

'Rubbish!'

'Well, it's too late now.'

Lorraine was clearly incensed. 'So—what do you intend doing now? You can't stay here.'

This was being frank with a vengeance! Julia shivered as she caught the look of sheer hatred on Lorraine's face. It took a lot of courage to retort calmly, 'Maybe not. But I will have to stay until I find something I really like.'

She didn't dare mention that she had promised Guy she would stay another six months. When it came to it, she hadn't the nerve to test Lorraine's restraint as far as that!

'You're impossible!' The open hatred in Lorraine's voice advised Julia that she had been wise to be cautious. Cruelly Lorraine jerked on her reins, bringing her spirited, pure-bred Arab horse up short. 'I'm going to find Guy. Does anyone know where he is?'

'*Oncle* Guy?' Fortune, mounting his pony while Julia held it, turned at the mention of his uncle's name. 'The last time I saw him he was in Julia's bedroom.'

'Julia's bedroom?' Lorraine's eyes widened in incredulous anger. 'You are telling the truth?'

'*Oui,*' he nodded. 'He was leaning out of her window. Fitz and I saw him from the garden.'

As Lorraine wheeled away, obviously furious, his small face puckered anxiously. 'Why is Lorraine cross, Julia?'

Need he ask! She had managed to recover her wits but still felt speechless at what Fortune had revealed. He and Lorraine had talked so quickly, she hadn't had a chance to get a word in, but she wasn't sure what she could have said if she had been able to. She couldn't have explained why Guy had been in her room and she hadn't had time to think of an adequate excuse.

'I wish you hadn't said anything about your uncle,' she faltered helplessly.

'Why not?' he asked, with childish directness.

'Oh, Fortune!' Julia sighed, shaking her head at him, while she suddenly remembered how the best form of defence was supposed to be attack. 'What were you doing in the garden at that hour, anyway? It was very early.'

'Nothing much,' Fortune muttered secretively.

'We were looking for the stork,' Fitz took the opportunity to grab the limelight for a change. 'When we couldn't find it we tried to see if it was sitting on a chimney. We've seen pictures of them sitting on chimneys.'

'What stork?' Julia asked suspiciously, not having seen one around.

'The one Hortense said the other day would be coming shortly!' they replied together.

Oh, no! Julia could have wept. The tale the boys had told Lorraine could lead to all sorts of complications, and the irony of it was that they wouldn't have been in the garden at all if Hortense had chosen to tell them the true facts of life instead of filling them with ridiculous stories about storks!

Later in the morning, when they caught up with Lorraine, they found her in a surprisingly good mood. She didn't seem pleased to see them and Julia had secretly hoped to avoid her, but there was nothing in her demeanour to suggest she'd had a row with Guy by confronting him about being in her bedroom. Julia shrewdly guessed she had had second thoughts over mentioning it, and if there were any thoughts of revenge in her head they wouldn't be directed at him. Lorraine was clever, she acknowledged wryly. She filled others with anxiety, then left them to stew in it while she went and enjoyed herself elsewhere.

Guy and his *gardiens* had spent the morning cutting some good bulls from the herds for forthcoming events in the arena, but were now ready to return to the house for lunch. As Julia and the twins reached where Guy and Lorraine were sitting on their horses in the shade of some trees, she couldn't help staring at him as he nodded a greeting. He wore a pair of dark trousers that fitted his powerful thighs and legs like a second skin, while his cotton shirt was open to the waist. Her glance lingered on the thick mat of dark hair thus revealed on his broad chest, and she had a sudden crazy urge to cross over to him and lay her cheek against it. He was as brown as any of his men and emitted such a blatant masculinity that she felt her face growing decidedly hot as he regarded her just as closely.

'Have you had a good ride?' he asked, his glance lingering on her silky shirt, as if he could see, only too well, that she wore nothing underneath. The morning had been hot and she had thought it would be more comfortable to wear as little as possible, and she hadn't expected to see anyone. All the same, she was sure she was quite decent! There was no need for him to look so disapproving.

'I might have enjoyed myself better if I'd been a better rider,' she said frankly, stroking her mount's neck apologetically.

'Where did you get to?'

'The boys wanted to see some wild horses and we found a herd in one of the marshes.'

Guy frowned. 'I'd rather you had waited until I had time to go with you.'

'You didn't say they were dangerous.'

'They aren't usually, but the stallions can be, when for some special reason they are guarding their mares.'

'All men are the same, are they not, *mon amour*?' Lorraine, laughing softly, leaned nearer him, coolly trailing a hand over his bare arm. As their horses were standing side by side she didn't have far to stretch, but both her action and words were suggestive enough to make Julia flush.

Guy appeared undisturbed by such forwardness, although Julia realised he could be responding underneath. He must care for Lorraine quite a lot, but he wasn't a man to wear his heart on his sleeve.

'You're embarrassing my young cousin,' he drawled mockingly, angering Julia by claiming a relationship he had so frequently denied.

He ought to be in public relations! she thought sourly as Lorraine laughed again, a sound which expressed such sheer satisfaction it set Julia's teeth on edge.

The men were forging ahead, having taken the twins

up in front of two of them, their ponies on lead ropes. Lorraine and Guy stirred their horses to follow while Julia trailed behind. If she kept well behind, she decided, she would at least be spared the pain of hearing them conversing softly with each other. She couldn't hear what they were saying, but judging from the grim glances Guy occasionally cast over his shoulder at her, he clearly regretted she was there at all!

It seemed to Julia, as the days passed, that she had lost more by refusing Léon's offer than she could ever have envisaged and the more she dwelt on it, the greater was her amazement at her own folly. Because Guy was domineering and considered her a part of his family, for no other reason, perhaps apart from personal prejudice, he didn't want her becoming a film star and at some future date maybe bringing a breath of scandal to his name. He had kissed her, now she knew in cold blood, until she had been willing to agree to anything. When she thought of how she had responded to his kisses on the way from Nice, she always broke into a cold sweat of sheer humiliation! What she ought to have done was to have packed her bags, after smacking his face, and gone straight back to Nice. By this time she would have made a start on her career for herself instead of being forced to endure the painful experience of having to live with a man who merely treated her as another responsibility, and daily demonstrated his indifference.

He still spent a lot of time with Lorraine and was taking her back to the coast, himself, when the twins returned home; Lorraine had asked him over dinner one evening if he wouldn't take a break and stay a few days when he was there. He had smiled at her and said he would think about it, which had seemed to Julia as good as a promise.

She had almost forgotten about André Tissier and was startled to meet him at a party. The party, oddly enough, it was given by some friends of Lorraine and she had— apparently with a continuing enthusiasm for olive branches—asked Julia to accompany her. Julia wasn't surprised to learn that Guy was going too, but he raised no objection to escorting both of them.

The party, held in the mansion home of a wealthy banker who lived near Marseilles, was already crowded with guests when they arrived. Marseilles, the third largest city in France after Paris and Lyons, was also a famous port, but they had bypassed this to reach Cassis, twelve miles to the east, from where Monsieur le Brun chose to commute each day. The views from the coast were wonderful, but it had grown too dark to see much.

Julia was wearing a white dress. She had thought of buying something a little more sophisticated until she recalled Guy's anger on the evening when she had worn her mother's black one. This, and remembering she was short of money, had made her settle for what was already in her wardrobe. The white dress with its spaghetti straps and bouffant skirt emphasising her narrow waist was very nice, she thought hopefully. She had brushed her honey-blonde hair until it gleamed and smoothed a hint of foundation over her smooth forehead, high cheekbones and straight nose. Her long silky lashes she had left alone and just used the lightest trace of lip-gloss. Her mouth looked too full and sensitive as it was without drawing attention to it.

Guy, in a dark velvet jacket, made the breath catch in her throat. He looked sensational—magnificent, moody, autocratic. Julia's mind was a confused mixture of words trying to describe him. He was so tall and dark, his classic features so clear-cut, any woman would have been proud to be seen with him. Tonight he was the suave sophisticate, with something of the international playboy image, yet Julia, with a flash of insight, knew she liked him as a rough Camargue cowboy best.

To her surprise, as they entered the banker's luxurious home, one of the first people she saw was André Tissier. 'André!' she exclaimed, as Guy released her arm which he had strangely kept hold of since leaving the car, much, Julia suspected, to Lorraine's annoyance. Julia hadn't appreciated the tightness of his grip which had disturbed her too much and made her feel threatened, and she welcomed André, when he approached, more warmly than she might otherwise have done. 'How lovely to see you,' she smiled.

André, appearing to believe she meant it, whisked her away. 'Come and have a drink and tell me what you've been doing with yourself,' he begged eagerly.

'Nothing much.' She didn't know the name of the drink he placed in her hand and glanced at it suspiciously.

'Don't worry,' he laughed. 'It's frothy but harmless.'

Like himself, she mused, then immediately felt ashamed.

'I've been trying to get hold of you,' he gazed at her intently, 'but every time I ring, Guy answers, and I get told you aren't available.'

Why should Guy tell him that? 'You must have rung when I was outside somewhere.'

'How would I know?' André shrugged. 'He never seems disposed to explain. Neither does he invite me to try again. If he wasn't so enamoured with the lovely Lorraine, I might have said he was jealous.'

'He's certainly not jealous,' Julia denied with a bright smile, which cost her an effort.

'Probably just over-protective?' André grinned optimistically, wanting to believe it. Julia's beauty had an unsettling influence when one saw the innocence behind it. It was a challenge to any red-blooded male and he didn't want another man interested in her. 'Fayme thinks he is.'

'Fayme?'

'*Oui*. She was disappointed when he wouldn't let you work for Léon, and that was one of the things she came up with.'

Julia frowned. Fayme and Léon must have been

surprised at Guy's anger after Léon had offered her a job and been able to reach no other conclusion. 'Well, despite Guy, we have managed to meet again,' she pointed out awkwardly. 'I didn't expect you to be here, though.'

'My parents are still away and they asked me to stand in for them,' he explained. 'They do not care to offend anyone as influential as le Brun, but most of the guests aren't of our generation. That's one of the reasons I was so pleased to see you.'

André was quite different from Pierre, Julia soon discovered. He was much livelier and more carefree. During the next hour he persuaded Julia to think about going to several functions with him, and she promised to let him know. Parties and festivals seemed to abound if one knew enough people and where to go to. It would be a relief to get away from Guy, if only for a few evenings. Otherwise she might never get over loving him.

She hadn't seen anything of him but when an overdose of André forced her to seek a brief respite on one of the terraces, Guy found her.

'Dance with me,' he said, looming above her.

She hesitated, reluctant to be that near him. 'I came out here to cool down.'

'Walk with me, then?' he smiled persuasively, and when Guy Guerard turned on the charm, Julia was unable to resist him. She might despise herself later, but the warm darkness and his dark presence was too tempting.

'Where did you meet André Tissier?' he asked idly, guiding her off the terrace along shadowy paths, 'Lorraine didn't introduce you.'

'He was at Fayme's house.'

'I see.' He paused and she could feel his eyes searching for hers in the moonlight. 'You like him?'

She kept her gaze steadily averted, not wanting him to guess André left her indifferent. 'How can I tell?' she shrugged evasively. 'I have to get to know him.'

'Do you want to?'

Julia sighed. She seemed to remember him asking the same questions about Pierre and she didn't want to waste precious moments talking about other men. 'Perhaps,' she replied.

His mouth tightened, Guy swung her to a halt beside a pool where a fountain played. 'Well,' he retorted sarcastically, 'now's your chance to spread your wings and find the excitement you crave. You won't find many parties smarter than this and there are plenty of men to choose from. Why settle for André?'

'Don't, Guy!' her face paled as the words fell from her nervous lips. 'I've told you, I don't want excitement or men. Just one would do . . .'

'Who?' he asked sharply, as her voice trailed off in consternation.

Drawing a shaky breath, she felt very young and breakable as she stood before him. Reality seemed to be fading, as it frequently did when they were alone together. 'What,' she asked dazedly, 'if it happened to be you?'

There was a peculiar pause in which his jaw went rigid, before he obviously decided to treat her query as a joke. A mocking smile touched his mouth. 'Are you by any chance trying to flirt with me, Julia?'

'I wouldn't dare.' Like a coward, she retreated, but was unable to meet his eyes. 'Sometimes when you get at me, I say things just to annoy you.'

'Why not be brave?' he laughed, as though he wasn't inclined to believe her.

He was laughing at her, not with her. The devil was in his voice, glittering from his eyes. Somehow his mockery hurt, yet it also goaded. Why shouldn't she flirt with him, as Lorraine did? When he kissed her she was always too overwhelmed by her own reactions to be able to judge his, but feminine intuition told her he wasn't as indifferent as he pretended to be. Although he had hinted that any attractive woman might arouse him, she thought it would take something more than that.

'Guy?' Deliberately she swayed against him and as her voice dropped huskily, she let her arms creep up around his neck. 'What do I have to do next? Beg?'

'No—never you,' he retorted thickly, gathering her close.

She hadn't expected him to take her seriously, but when, suddenly panic-stricken, she tried to release herself he didn't allow second thoughts.

'Oh, no, you don't,' he muttered, lowering his head.

The quality of his kiss was different, yet somehow the same as before. His mouth held a similar, urgent passion, but each time their lips met it was like the first time, only more intense. There seemed always a wild merging of the senses. For Julia it was something which developed rapidly to a devastating hunger demanding to be assuaged. And what ever it was, her confused mind assured her, between them there would always be a clamouring for more.

'Satisfied?' she heard his voice, low on her bruised lips, and in a shameless haze she whispered, 'No.'

'Julia, *pour l'amour de Dieu!*' he groaned, touching his lips to hers again, brushing them backwards and forwards until her own parted helplessly. His mouth was unbelievably soft, one moment, taut and demanding the next, and while he continued kissing her, his hands caressed her body tormentingly, arousing a shattering desire in her lower limbs as he pressed her savagely against him. She was aware of every hard-muscled inch of him and knew instinctively they were a mere breath away from becoming one. It was a strange, unearthly sensation. She felt she was lost, drowning in emotion and unable to save herself.

'The grass is dry,' Guy muttered hoarsely, nibbling her ear.

He had assessed the extent of her involvement which she couldn't hide. Desire lay so thick between them as to be almost visible, and the silent currents rushing through their entwined bodies was something it wasn't possible to fight. Julia realised she was shaking, but her hands clutched tighter as she nodded, giving a silent, fevered assent to the question he didn't need to ask.

Then they were interrupted. As Guy's arms actually tightened to lift her, Lorraine called his name.

'Guy, *mon chéri*! Where are you?'

Julia shivered as he stepped away from her, the swiftness of his movement betraying his embarrassment, filling her with humiliation.

Driving home, Julia admitted she might have reason to be grateful to Lorraine. She had rushed up to them, babbling some story about their host wanting to speak to Guy, although she hadn't batted an eyelid when they had returned to find Le Brun happily circulating among his guests without any apparent recollection of having anything urgent to discuss with anyone!

Perhaps Guy had guessed this. He had gone straight back to the house, but he hadn't hurried. Julia realised that while he had seen through Lorraine's ploy he had gratefully made use of it.

What would have happened under the trees if she had listened to his persuasions? Not that she really believed they would have gone that far. What had taken place between them had merely proved he wasn't immune to the sense-drugging atmosphere of the garden. In the warmth of a semi-tropical night, he had briefly allowed the sensuous side of his nature to take over.

Staring at the rigid lines of his dark, handsome head—for she was, as she usually was when Lorraine was present, in the back of the car—Julia suspected Guy was a man with a deeply passionate nature. A controlled one, as she knew only too well, but a man who, when he allowed his control to slip, would be a very demanding lover. One whom a girl of her naïve innocence could perhaps never hope to satisfy, even if she were married to him.

When André got in touch again, asking her to a party, she accepted, knowing that at long last there was only one way she could help herself, and if she didn't succeed she would at least have the comfort of knowing she had tried.

'Enjoying yourself?' Guy's voice halted her at two o'clock one morning after André had brought her home. Coming from the study, he intercepted her, and she paused with a foot on the stairs.

Defensively her hand flew to her rumpled hair. She realised she must look untidy, but André's car was an open sports and she had forgotten her scarf.

'Your lipstick needs attention too,' he remarked coldly.

She flushed, staring at him resentfully. 'That's because I haven't used any since I left.'

'Not because André said goodnight too enthusiastically?'

His eyes on her bare mouth were so contemptuous she squirmed, yet at the same time he made her angry. 'Just because Lorraine's gone it doesn't mean we all have to live like hermits!'

'*Mon Dieu*! If I thought you were really serious!'

Her feet jerked another step upwards. It took her a safer distance from him while giving her the advantage of being nearer his height. Then she regretted moving at all, for she could also see more clearly the fury in his eyes.

'I'm tired, Guy.' Like a coward, the fight went out of her.

'I wonder why!'

He knew how to hurt, didn't he just! The picture he painted with merely one disdainful glance was better than many an artist might have achieved with a canvas and brush! 'You shouldn't judge us all by your own standards!' she cried, insensed.

'Why, you little . . .' As his hand went swiftly out to grasp her, with a fury which stated rather than hinted that he didn't give a damn for the consequences, Hortense came to the top of the stairs.

'Guy—*monsieur*!' she appealed with her hands. 'You know Madame has had one of her heads! I've just left her and she is sleeping soundly, but for how much longer, if this commotion goes on, I should not like to say!'

How much longer, Julia wondered, reaching her bedroom, after taking advantage of the housekeeper's reproving presence, would she be able to escape the full force of his anger, which she seemed so constantly to be provoking by the sharpness of her tongue. Recalling the unleashed fury in his eyes, she refused to guess. If she wasn't careful she would find herself turning into a shrew! Guy had no right to accuse her of behaving less than decorously with the men she went out with, but how could she accuse him of being insulting when she insulted him back?

Feeling suddenly too weary to try and sort it out, Julia tore off her clothes, then flinging herself down on her bed began to weep.

CHAPTER EIGHT

THE house was quiet, with Lorraine and the twins gone, much too quiet for someone reluctant to be alone with their thoughts. Julia occupied herself helping Hortense and her aunt, but there were long periods, while Mavis was resting when she wasn't needed. André was becoming increasingly attentive and she shamelessly encouraged him, while realising she was only using him as a diversion. There were times when she felt she couldn't bear the mysterious pressures building up inside herself, and she used André as a means of getting away from Champonale.

Despite not knowing whether Guy really approved of André or not, she continued to go out with him. He was good company and he didn't complain when, as she suspected, she sometimes wasn't. He had little of Pierre's reticence, yet he never objected too forcibly when she refused to kiss him, other than lightly as they said goodnight.

That he appeared to have a proper respect for her made her suspect he was growing serious about her, so she wasn't unduly surprised when he asked her to marry him. He had brought her home one evening, late as usual, and she was half asleep when he proposed.

'I have good prospects, *mon amie*,' he said softly, his confidence revealing alarmingly that he had every hope of being accepted. 'I would make you a good husband, *chérie*, one of the best.'

This did wake Julia up. 'What time is it?' she gasped, blinking at him, hoping futilely she had merely been dreaming.

André smiled, gently teasing. 'Is time important when

a man is proposing? Surely it can't be of any consequence when I'm telling a girl that I love her?'

How easy he made it seem, how simple. There was only one snag, Julia thought hollowly; he wasn't the right man for her. But then the one she wanted didn't want her. She would be crying for the moon, wasting her life if she waited for him! Even so, she couldn't bring herself to accept André's proposal immediately.

'I haven't met your parents yet,' she protested.

'Julia!' he exclaimed imperiously. 'I don't have to seek their permission, or rely on what they think!'

No, he wouldn't. She smiled at him wanly. He was almost thirty and, according to odd whispers which had reached her ears, his despairing mother would give anything to see him married to almost any girl.

'My parents would happily settle for anyone,' André laughed, as if he had read her thoughts. More dryly he added, 'It is important to them that I settle down and provide them with grandchildren to ensure the succession!'

That was one thing she liked about André, his quick sense of humour, though it could be a little unkind. And occasionally the barbed wit of his tongue could be irritating. Suddenly she clenched her hands, aghast that she could even be contemplating marrying a man whom she not only didn't love, but whose manners she didn't always approve of. It wouldn't be fair to either of them—and yet the one chance she might get to escape Guy and Champonale was surely not to be rejected out of hand?

'You'll have to give me time,' she said weakly. 'Why not wait until your parents come home?'

'You haven't seen my home.'

She hadn't, and he wasn't asking a question. She waited for him to go on.

'It's near Guy's other estate in the Rhone valley, where viticulture is the main topic of conversation. Do you know much about the wines of the Côtes du Rhone?' he asked with faint amusement.

'Not a lot,' she admitted. Happier to be on what she considered safer ground, she said eagerly, 'But I would love to learn.'

'There's a great deal to learn,' he said soberly, making her suspect he took his home and occupation a great deal more seriously than he pretended to.

'I could help.'

'Help?'

'At the vintage—isn't it called? The grape-picking.'

To Julia's bewilderment, André threw back his head and laughed. *'Ma belle,'* he spluttered wryly, 'how I adore you! I offer you my hand and heart, and you are more interested in the grape!'

Suddenly, as though to prove that didn't interest him most, he grabbed hold of her and kissed her.

Feeling his lips on her own, Julia shivered with a quick revulsion which apparently André mistook for nervousness.

'Ah,' he murmured tenderly, releasing her. 'So shy— but I can wait.'

Why should he? Julia thought morosely, a few days later, after she had endured the scorching whiplash of Guy's tongue. His temper had become worse lately— sometimes she felt she was living on the edge of a volcano. Only yesterday he had literally dragged her from her horse, in front of his men, making her cheeks scorch, and all because she hadn't guessed a storm was brewing. He hadn't even apologised when the storm didn't arrive—he had merely snapped, when reproached, that it might have done.

The weather was terribly hot and she knew that a storm, rare though it might be in these parts, could be devastating. But she was sure Guy needn't have been so rough with her. She still bore the marks of his hands on her bare arms, could still feel his furious breath on her face.

It was because he was missing Lorraine, she supposed, and was suffering. Julia fell to imagining all kinds of things, such as Lorraine issuing ultimatums. 'Get rid of your cousin—who isn't a cousin,' she might have said. 'or I won't marry you.' The solution, Julia decided miserably, was to release Guy from a promise he must regret more each day by marrying herself to a man who adored her too much to notice she didn't adore him. André's ardour, already showing signs of getting out of hand, should be more than enough for the two of them.

Guy was, in fact, going to his other estate for a few days.

'Why don't you come with him and stay with us?' André wheedled over the telephone, when she told him. 'My parents should be back by then and you can discover all the secrets of wine-making.'

She guessed that if she went he would demand a straight answer to his proposal, a decision she had feverishly kept putting off. 'The vintage isn't until September,' she replied, with what she realised must be an infuriating lack of enthusiasm.

'There are other things to be decided before then,' he said firmly, clearly hinting that he wouldn't allow her to prevaricate for ever.

'I'll ask Guy,' she promised unhappily.

'No!' Guy refused, very emphatically.

'Why not?' Julia pleaded, holding on to her temper, because she hadn't expected to get her own way without an argument. He pandered to her whims very little. Where once he had been fairly tolerant he was becoming increasingly impatient. 'Why not?' she repeated, as his mouth merely thinned.

'For reasons I shouldn't have to explain,' his dark eyes were hard and unyielding, 'André's parents haven't met you, and they are away.'

'They're coming back.'

'But if they were still away when you arrived?'

'Well, what of it?' Her entrancing chin rose stubbornly. 'There'll be other people around.'

'Perhaps, but there's no guarantee, and I won't expose you to that kind of risk.'

'You're just being awkward!' she muttered, wondering unhappily why he had no idea she was doing this entirely for his sake.

'No.' Her choice of words obviously displeased him, but he didn't openly rebuke her. His next cutting comment, however, did. 'I have neither the time nor money to spare for the immediate wedding convention would demand were you to spend the night alone with André Tissier.'

'I'm sure you must have spent the night alone with a—a woman,' she stammered pointedly.

'That,' he retorted curtly, 'is an entirely different matter and needn't concern you.'

Julia found his cool aloofness infuriating. 'But it's the same thing.'

His mouth hard, he shook his head. 'I have never taken advantage of a *jeune fille*, especially a virgin.'

Hating to think of him making love to anyone, Julia choked, 'Aren't you being old-fashioned?'

'Perhaps I am.' His eyes flickered coldly over her flushed, defiant face. 'Good advice is often considered old-fashioned, but if you had the whole district pointing a finger at you for immoral behaviour, you might wish you had listened.'

'So,' glaring at him, she sucked in a dry breath, 'if I defy you and stay with André, I'm liable to be branded a scarlet woman?'

'Not exactly.' His voice had a silky edge to it. 'If the couple involved marry, people eventually forgive and forget, but you aren't going anywhere—and that's an order!'

For the rest of the day Julia stayed in her room, rendered almost ill by the depth of her misery. She could see clearly the decision she had to make, and although it was the last thing she wanted to do, she realised she had no alternative but to tell Guy of

André's proposal and announce that she was going to marry him. She ought to have told Guy this morning instead of foolishly trying to avoid committing herself. It had been stupid to imagine André's parents might offer her a job, almost as incredible as it had been to believe Léon could turn her into a film star overnight. It was no use hiding her head in the sand any longer. Unless she wanted to remain here and see Guy living with Lorraine, she would have to find every bit of courage she could muster—and use it!

Having come to a definite decision, Julia daren't give herself a chance to change her mind. In the early evening she sought Guy out, finding him in one of the huge barns. The cavernous doors stood open to the sun, but the rear of the building was shadowy in places where the sun didn't reach. Until he spoke she thought he wasn't there, but following the direction of his voice, she saw him standing against one of the black old beams, looking about as strong and impregnable. As usual when he worked, his shirt was unbuttoned to the waist, his trousers tight, making her swallow.

'Guy?'

'Julia?' he frowned at her uneven tones. 'You want me?'

Didn't he know how much! Closing her eyes, as a wild surge of emotion rushed through her, she nodded blindly.

'Then come out of the sun,' he suggested coolly.

She advanced slowly, halting nearer to him. She suddenly felt too hot, her cotton dress clinging. 'I have to talk to you.'

As if he'd heard enough for one day, Guy replied indifferently, 'I'm busy.'

'How encouraging!' Her mouth twisted.

'Couldn't whatever you want to talk about wait?' he asked dryly. 'After this morning I doubt if we're in the mood to be *sympathique* with each other.'

Julia agreed, but realised it was now or never.

Perhaps the glint in his eye, denoting the slight humour of a man confident of his superior male strength, drove her on. 'I've decided to marry André, *monsieur*.'

Ignoring her formality, which she used to aid complete detachment, he was silent. On raising her eyes to his face, Julia saw he had gone quite pale. For another strained moment he stared at her, then said tersely, 'I think not.'

'You—think not?' Too bewildered to be angry, her eyes widened. 'But, *monsieur*, wasn't it your idea that I should marry, in the first place? When I first came here you said . . .'

Like a knife he cut in. 'Have you spoken to André today?'

'No . . .'

'Then I suggest you're making this up,' he countered curtly, 'otherwise you would have mentioned it earlier. You would have said then that you were going to marry him instead of prattling on about merely going to stay with him.'

'But he has asked me to marry him,' she stammered, protesting. 'Since this morning, I've been giving it more thought.'

'Well, you can think again.'

'*Monsieur . . . !*'

'Please drop that ridiculous title! And stop trying to fool me. You've been in your room for hours.' His eyes bored ruthlessly into her. 'You didn't come down for lunch. You were too busy, I imagine, planning your next move. André hasn't asked you to marry him, but you decided to twist the warning I gave you to your own advantage. You are now attempting to deceive me into allowing you to visit him in the hope of forcing him to marry you. This would naturally create all the stimulation which your shallow little soul craves.'

'How dare you!' she choked.

Guy laughed openly at her shocked expression. '*Mon*

Dieu, what an actress! I should have let Léon have you, after all.'

As her hand shot out to slap the mockery from his face, he caught it savagely, but she was past noticing the pain. 'André did propose . . .'

'What?'

'And he did ask me to visit him. You can be as insulting as you like!'

'Don't you think I would have checked?'

Julia drew a sobbing breath, finding such a bitter exchange utterly exhausting. 'You have my permission to check all you please.'

'Calling my bluff, are you?' he snapped harshly. 'Maybe you're right and, unfortunately, in this instance, too damned clever. If I asked André if he has proposed to my ward, it puts us both in an awkward position. He may have intentions, but not ones he'd care to repeat to me!'

Julia sighed, suddenly too miserable to argue. 'You've got it all wrong . . .'

'Some of it, perhaps,' he agreed. 'There are many sides to a relationship—I don't profess to be an expert. But I don't wish to hear any more about yours with other men, not while I'm responsible for you.'

'Does that mean,' she glanced at him dully, 'that I'm not to go out with anyone?'

'Go out with whom you like,' his eyes glittered darkly as he flung her numb hand away and made to stride past her. 'Just as long as you spare me the details!'

White and totally bewildered, Julia returned to her room, after letting Hortense know she still wasn't feeling well and wouldn't require any dinner. When Hortense protested that she might feel worse if she didn't eat anything, she agreed without interest to having soup and coffee sent up.

Sheer desperation, during the next few days, drove Julia into conceiving a plan she would never otherwise have contemplated. Guy grimly ignored her, although she had resumed eating downstairs and willed herself to act normally. His temper didn't improve, and when she tried to be friendly he didn't respond. Sometimes he stared at her so coldly she was sure he must hate her.

Lorraine, too, made her feel very bitter. One day she happened to answer the telephone when the other girl rang, but when she had offered to seek Guy, Lorraine had forbidden her sharply to do so. After muttering that it wasn't Guy she wanted to speak to, she had let loose a stream of abuse on Julia's helpless head. Julia had been forced to listen while Lorraine had accused her of continuing to be a nuisance that no one knew what to do about, and how Guy was almost at his wits' end.

As this tallied with his present attitude, Julia found it impossible to discredit what Lorraine had said. She grew increasingly hurt and angry and had suddenly known what she must do. The idea had come to her through the night, as she had lain awake, tears drying on her cheeks. It might be deceitful, but it was the only way she could think of which would almost guarantee her escape.

Guy was leaving, the next day, for his other estate up the lonely reaches of the Rhone valley, and she decided to go with him, though he wouldn't know it. She would hide in the back of the truck he was taking, which was already packed with various items of equipment. She had heard him telling Mavis, during dinner, that he hoped to leave some time the following evening.

This suited Julia's rough plan very well, as she intended hiding in the back of the truck after pretending she was going to stay overnight with a girl friend, who was picking her up. Then, when they reached Guy's other house, which was apparently not used during his absence, Julia planned to sneak out and hide. She reckoned that shouldn't be too difficult, as it would be dark and there would be no one about. Mavis had mentioned that the only person who came to the house was the overseer's wife, who cooked meals for Guy, when he required them.

Julia was determined she would get into the house somehow and manage to keep out of sight until the next morning. She wasn't quite sure what she would do then. She hoped to have enough nerve to sneak into Guy's bed, after he had gone out, and allow his manager's wife to discover her when she came to tidy his room after breakfast.

She wasn't sure either what might occur after that, but if all Guy had said was true, and she had no reason to suspect it wasn't, he would have to either marry her or send her away. Julia smiled to herself grimly, with a kind of dull triumph. As he would never marry her, the only course open to him would be to send her away. She could see it all happening, like the sequence of a play, one which people declared could never happen in real life. Guy wouldn't be able to get her back to England fast enough. She preferred not to think of his fury while convincing herself that she might easily persuade him to make her a loan until she found a job, when she would repay him, of course. There was just a chance, she believed that some money from her father's estate might have at last reached a bank in London. The last communication Guy had received about this had been quite hopeful. Perhaps all she would need was a loan to get home.

If the next day had been a normal one and she'd had more time to think about it, Julia doubted if she would have gone ahead with such a reckless scheme. As it turned out, Mavis kept her extra busy all morning and talked a lot about a party she hoped to make up for a visit to the famous Avignon Festival in July.

'You'll enjoy it, dear,' she smiled gently. 'I'm so glad you'll be here.'

Mavis so rarely went out and Julia felt tears dampen her eyes as the exclamation of delight she felt forced to give made her feel terribly guilty. 'Does Guy go?' she asked, as usual eager to talk about him, this time aware she wouldn't be able to much longer.

'Occasionally,' Mavis nodded. 'This year, I believe, Lorraine is going with him. If she does, I imagine it won't be long before their engagement is announced.'

That was enough to remove the last lingering doubts from Julia's mind regarding the wisdom of what she had planned. And, amazingly, even fate seemed disposed to help her. After lunch she decided to take a rest as she didn't dare risk falling asleep in Guy's truck and making a noise that might betray her presence.

Possibly because she rarely slept in the afternoon, she woke later than she had intended, but when she rushed downstairs, instead of finding Guy already gone, Mavis, to her relief, told her that he had been unexpectedly called away and when he returned would have to leave for l'Ejienne immediately.

A little later, pretending she would walk down the road to meet the friend who was picking her up, Julia slipped from the house. She had chosen a time when she knew the men wouldn't be around, to find Guy's truck and hide in the back, under a pile of old sacking. The sacks were dry and dusty and the dust irritated her nose. It wasn't very comfortable—but she hadn't imagined it would be.

She had allowed for everything but the additional tension of waiting for Guy to arrive. It was only an hour, but it seemed more like five, before he came and they set off. Feeling tense with nerves, stiff from lying in an unnatural position and threatened by cramp, Julia began to regret what she was doing before they had got very far. It was only by constantly reminding herself that Guy was going to marry Lorraine that she was able to stick it out.

He drove the whole way without stopping, but it was still late when they reached l'Ejienne. Julia had resisted every impulse to look at him, fearing he might hear if she moved, and while the journey had seemed interminable she guessed the worst was yet to come. Tension made her feel so ill she wondered if she was going to be sick, and, suddenly terrified this might happen, she pressed a shaking hand over her mouth.

Almost at once, when Guy pulled up, there were voices greeting him. Daring to ease a corner of the sacking, Julia heard a man speaking to him. Faintly she made out that someone called Monique had a meal waiting for him, but in their own home, as they had assumed he would be hungry but hadn't known what time he would arrive.

She heard Guy thanking him, admitting he was hungry and appreciated the trouble Monique had gone to. From the warmer tone of his voice, Julia gathered he had much regard for Bernard—as he called him—and his wife. When Bernard enquired about the unpacking of the truck, Julia trembled with relief when Guy replied that there was nothing that couldn't wait until the morning. This was one of the moments she had been dreading, for she had known that, if Guy had ordered otherwise, she would soon have been discovered. She said a silent prayer of thanksgiving as they walked away.

As their voices faded, Julia eased herself carefully from her hiding place and looked cautiously around. There was a moon, but it wasn't bright, so she could see little. The house loomed big and dark, more château-like than Champonale, and the truck appeared to be parked right outside the front door. She waited until she was sure Guy and Bernard had gone, then crept inside.

Again it was easier than she had anticipated. The door wasn't locked and she closed it quickly behind her, grateful that she hadn't been forced to climb in through a window. The huge hall was in darkness, though, and she hadn't allowed for the strangeness of the atmosphere. The old house appeared to be watching her, making odd little sounds in its throat, its face full of shadows.

Telling herself not to be so fanciful, Julia paused. She

was really too anxious to be nervous. As her eyes grew
adjusted, she crept up the stairs which she could just
discern in the filtering moonlight. Her heart was beating
loudly as she reached the top. In a state of panic she
suddenly realised she didn't know which bedroom
belonged to Guy.

Cursing her own foolishness, she gazed around,
trying to penetrate the gloom. It would have been easy
enough to have got the information from Mavis, if
she'd been tactful. Not only had she to find somewhere
to sleep, she had to find where Guy slept so she could
easily find his room in the morning.

Fortunately she found his room first. It was so
obviously the master suite, the bed made up and turned
down, waiting, that she didn't look any further. She
found a small room for herself at the other end of the
corridor, with a bathroom next door. In the room stood
a narrow single bed covered by a single blanket. Apart
from this it contained only a rough wooden dressing-
table and mirror. It was bare and plain, but for Julia a
most welcome sight, since she was certain it was a place
which the master of the house would never enter.

But by the time she returned from the bathroom she
was shaking with nerves again. She was so frightened
she sat on the floor behind the door, for fear he took it
into his head to check the house before he retired. Now
she had got this far, her courage was rapidly failing. She
couldn't even be sure she would still have enough to
carry out her plan in the morning.

It must have been midnight when she heard him
come in. His footsteps came swiftly up the stairs and as
the door of his suite closed, she breathed a sigh of relief
and lay down on the bed, having already wrapped
herself in the warm blanket. She had removed all her
clothes except her silky bra and panties and the blanket
tickled her skin unbearably. In the end, she had to
throw it off before she could get to sleep.

Later, when something woke her, she couldn't

immediately recall where she was. She had no awareness of anything but danger. Like a small wild animal she was conscious of fear and an instinctive desire to hide. She still had her eyes closed and there was nothing in the silence surrounding her to warn her, when she opened them, that she would find Guy standing in the doorway, watching her.

As her horrified glance met his, he asked derisively, 'I suppose you have a good explanation?'

She had to swallow several times before she could answer, and each time it was more painful. Every part of her appeared to be frozen and for a moment his question seemed to have no relevance. Instead of answering him, she asked hoarsely, 'How did you discover I was here?'

Despite his obvious fury, he answered her question first. 'Intuition,' he replied shortly and grimly. 'I woke feeling something was wrong. I suddenly knew I wasn't in the house alone and when I opened my bedroom door I heard someone sneezing, which rather confirmed it. The dust which you'd inhaled in the back of the truck must have been bothering you.'

Contemptuously his eyes roamed over her, making her remember belatedly how little she had on. Flushing scarlet, she wrapped herself clumsily in the blanket she had been lying on. 'If you know so much,' she whispered apprehensively, 'why bother to ask?'

Leaning his rigid length against the door-jamb, Guy pushed his hands in his pockets, without removing his hard gaze from her hot face. 'I'm asking why—not how! There was only one way you could have got here.'

Julia looked at him furtively over the top of the blanket. He was wearing an old dressing-gown that barely covered his powerful body and obviously nothing underneath. Her heart began beating unsteadily as his dark virility hit her like a blow.

'Perhaps I came for the ride . . .' she muttered, trying to hide her growing awareness with a careless shrug.

Guy had every right to be furious with her, she thought despairingly. She even felt furious herself when she realised what a mess she had made of everything. If only she'd had the sense to stay awake, she might have been able to prevent herself from sneezing, or at least she could have hidden her head under the blanket and muffled the sound.

'So you came for the ride?' he said with a deceptive gentleness.

'Why not?' she hedged warily.

'You told Mavis you were going to a party and would stay overnight with the Renauds.'

'I know . . .' She really did feel ashamed about that, but what was occupying her mind most at the moment was the problem of finding a convincing excuse, not for deceiving Mavis but for coming here. She wasn't so stupid as to believe Guy would accept that she had merely come along for the fun of it.

'I would have checked if I hadn't been in such a hurry,' she heard him saying, 'but I suppose that was a risk you were prepared to take?'

'I didn't think you would be interested enough to bother,' she replied, quite truthfully.

'Right!' He made every pulse in her body jump by abandoning his lounging position by the door and striding over to sit on the edge of her bed, almost on top of her. 'That's got the incidentals out of the way, so now we can get down to the basics—and I want the truth!'

'The—the truth?' she stammered, keeping her gaze trained apprehensively on the front of his dressing-gown. Her heart, still beating unsteadily, quickened in sheer terror. She could see his chest rising and falling as if he only contained his anger with difficulty, and she shrank as far from him as she could.

'Haven't you heard of it?' he snapped, with no obvious pity for the dilemma she was in.

There seemed only one story she could stick to with any hope of success, and feebly she produced it. 'If you must know,' she muttered, 'I was curious to see what kind of place you had here.'

'Do you think I'm stupid?'

She retreated further, until she was right against the wall. She felt completely helpless, since there was no way she could tell him the truth.

'You came because of Tissier, didn't you?' Guy's accusation stunned her, taking her completely by surprise although it shouldn't have done, but she had forgotten all about André. 'You were going to him?'

'No!' she gasped frantically, wondering if he would try and stop her if she begged to be allowed to go to the bathroom where she could lock the door and climb through the window and simply run away.

'I shouldn't try it, if I were you,' he said furiously.

Having no means of knowing if he had read her thoughts or was referring to André, she stared at him wordlessly. He looked suddenly dangerous. His hair was rumpled and his dark, chiselled features looked harder and more ruthless than she could ever remember seeing them.

When she didn't reply but lay gazing at him, her eyes too big for her face, he bent over her, taunting silkily, 'What would you have gone to André Tissier for? Love, excitement, notoriety? The last I could give you, if you're desperate, I could certainly supply the other two. A kind of loving, anyway, and more pleasure than you might be able to take!'

Julia glared at him, her temper rising again as his eyes travelled over her, insolently measuring every curve. Although she was wrapped in a blanket, she felt he could see through it, and the way her skin tingled made her cringe with shame. 'I don't want anything from either you or any other man!'

'Well, of course, what else could you say?' he mocked contemptuously.

'You'll have to let me go!' He wasn't touching her, but she felt as imprisoned as if he had her in chains.

'No,' he murmured, smoothly menacing, 'you aren't going anywhere until I've finished with you.'

Her cheeks went hot, then paled as his weight shifted and her nerves tightened like bow-strings as she tried to anticipate his next move.

'Can't we talk?' she whispered hoarsely, clinging hopefully to the old adage about soft words turning away wrath.

'It wasn't talking I had in mind,' he said unpleasantly, his hands flashing out to seize her, pulling her to him with iron intensity.

The swiftness of his attack threw her off balance and for a horrifying moment she thought she was going to faint. 'Don't touch me!' she cried, beginning to struggle as his lips found hers with bruising force and her mouth was crushed beneath his in a long, brutal kiss.

'Don't fight me,' he muttered savagely, with obviously no intention of doing as she asked.

At first his hard cruelty appalled her, but suddenly, as the urgency of his kisses increased, she was helpless against the frightening desire which started surging through her veins. She felt she was sinking in warm, swirling waters and was having to cling to him to keep from drowning.

She was aware of every movement of his lean body as his arms bound her tightly to him, and a suffocating sensation seemed to be melting away the last of her resistance. When he pushed aside the blanket which confined her to free the catch on her bra, she drew a sharp breath, which she lost completely as his hands closed inexorably over the tender fullness of her breasts.

Suddenly it was too late for either of them. As his hands touched her breasts she knew dazedly that he had passed the point of control. She didn't recognise herself either. Her senses were reeling under a kind of wild ecstasy which unrelentingly took over.

Even so, it was a shock when Guy lifted her and carried her to his own room. She began to tremble as he laid her on his bed. The sheets were smooth beneath her, in direct contrast to the rough mat of curling hair on his chest as he threw off his dressing gown and drew her back into his arms.

'What are you going to do with me?' she gasped, on a brief note of returning sanity.

'*Ma chérie,*' he replied, the bitter anger in his voice making her shrink, 'you should have asked yourself that before you came here, should you not?'

CHAPTER NINE

WHEN Guy began kissing her again, Julia lay trying to steady her leaping pulses and trying to think. It was impossible, and too late. While she did make another attempt to get away from him, his ravaging kisses filled her with warm, sensual feelings she couldn't fight. Soon she was overwhelmed by an irresistible yearning to respond to him and give him everything he desired. As his mouth explored every inch of her face, she caught a glimpse of his eyes burning like red-hot coals and she knew, with a fatalistic indifference, that he was speaking the truth when he muttered thickly, 'I can't stop now.'

Exposed to the experienced insistence of his lips, Julia was swept breathlessly to another world, one that contained only themselves, where nothing existed but sensation. Her mouth became soft and incredibly responsive under his and aware of her surrender, he began slowly caressing the surging contours of her breasts, his fingers leaving trails of fire on her hardening nipples. She could feel his heart pounding and the heat searing her from his hard body.

When their lips fused in violent passion, for Julia at least, coherent thought was gone. She didn't realise that the tight grip of her arms, the searching eagerness of her slender limbs were giving the impression that she was far from innocent. Having lost all real consciousness of what was happening, she was at the mercy of her basically passionate nature. When Guy's hands slid under her, lifting her to him, she was delighted rather than shocked by the naked urgency of his body.

It wasn't until he possessed her that she was jerked ruthlessly from the exciting new world in which she had been floating, into a frightening welter of pain and shock. Her cry of agony was shrill but lost against the pressure of his mouth. She lay beneath him, entirely helpless, feeling battered by a raging storm and not least by her own emotions. Her heart was thudding wildly in panicky fear, but when she began to twist and turn in an effort to escape him, her wild defiance only seemed to inflame him. His weight pressed her into the mattress while his lips forced her clenched teeth apart and his steely hands caught her threshing ones, holding them captive above her head.

After that it was soon over, as a rush of sensation carried them both to explosive heights and complete fulfilment. Through drumming ears, Julia heard his hoarse groan, his breath catch in a rough, inarticulate exclamation, as if he was gripped by feelings too strong to be manageable. She had a brief impression of his eyes like flames, then all was silent.

When he rolled away from her, Julia thought her eyes were too hot and dry for tears, and she was dully surprised to find them running down her cheeks. With a half-smothered sob, she allowed them to take over, burying her face in a pillow. In a short time she felt Guy stir, but she knew bitterly he wouldn't be crying! He wouldn't waste even a sigh of regret, let alone a tear, over a girl who he would consider had got exactly what she deserved.

She was sure she could have killed him, yet when he left the bed she felt strangely vulnerable and suddenly longed to be back in his arms. But he made no attempt to touch her again, and his voice when it came offered no comfort. It was so curt that she couldn't believe the regret he pretended to feel.

'I didn't mean this to happen, Julia. Not this way.'

'Are there different ways?' She kept her face hidden, but her misery and rage was expressed quite clearly through her voice. 'You were cruel!'

Throwing his dressing-gown on, he sat down beside

her, turning her over, his hands gentle but forceful as he made her look at him. As he studied her wet cheeks intently she wondered how he could act as though nothing had happened. He was pale, but the cool arrogance was back in his face, easily replacing his former passion.

'That was your first time,' he said starkly, a muscle jerking in his jaw. 'I could say a lot more, but I'm not going to. There are more important things to do and discuss, and we must hurry.'

He was going too fast for her. 'What do you mean?' she asked numbly, trying frantically now to stem her tears.

Guy hesitated, his glance touching the bruised tenderness of her mouth and body as if he couldn't help himself. Something flared darkly in the depth of his eyes, reminding her of how he had been a few minutes ago. As her breath caught the back of her throat his expression changed. 'Are you feeling all right?' he asked abruptly.

He might have been a motorist enquiring politely after the health of a pedestrian he'd just flattened! He was so impersonal, Julia shivered. 'Yes,' she replied, willing to die rather than admit she wasn't.

He frowned slightly. 'Then you must dress.'

'Don't worry,' she burst out, 'you needn't be worried that I'll stay here and embarrass you!' Feverishly she struggled to cover herself up. 'I'll be gone before you realise, if you'd kindly bring my clothes.'

'Julia!' he spoke softly, but the command in his voice silenced her. 'Will you please listen? We're both leaving, the sooner the better. Where do you think you'd be going on your own?'

While she digested this, he left the room, but returned quickly with her jeans. Dropping them beside her, he commanded tautly, 'Get into these, then wait for me downstairs until I've cleaned up here. I'd rather my manager's wife didn't suspect anything.'

As he cynically turned his back, Julia scrambled to do as she was told. She stumbled twice before reaching the door, but when Guy asked if she was sure she was all right, she merely nodded. She felt too distraught to enquire what he intended doing next, and suddenly she didn't care. Any respect and affection he had had for her was gone, and it was a bitter pill to swallow that it was entirely her own fault!

Because she went first to the bathroom, by the time she got downstairs she discovered he had beaten her to it and was coming from the kitchen with a cup of steaming coffee in his hand.

'Have this,' he said coldly. 'You must need something, and we've got a long journey ahead of us again.'

'Us?' holding the cup unsteadily, she looked at him blankly.

Carefully he took a note from his pocket, placing it on a nearby table. 'This is for Monique. She will find it in the morning when she comes to tidy the house and cook my breakfast. It will inform her that for personal reasons, I have decided to return to Champonale for a few days, but will be coming back . . .' he paused, staring straight at Julia, 'I didn't add—for my honeymoon.'

Julia swayed, her face white. 'Oh, no!' she groaned inwardly, he had decided to marry Lorraine at last and was bringing her here. How could he, after what had happened! 'With Lorraine,' she whispered.

'With you,' he snapped.

'With—me?' Incredibly hurt by his cruel joke, she gripped the back of a chair. 'Do you realise what you're saying?'

'I do, if you don't,' he retorted. 'You have to understand that you're my bride-to-be. We are returning to Champonale at once and I will pretend to have picked you up from the Renauds' party. I will imply that I can do without you no longer and that we are to be married immediately.'

On top of everything else it was too much! It had taken more courage than she had known she possessed to come downstairs and face Guy, but now she felt desperate. How could she allow Guy to sacrifice himself over something for which *she* had been mostly responsible?

'But Lorraine——?' she began.

'I have never discussed marriage with Lorraine.'

Hysteria edged its way into Julia's throat, she had to struggle to contain it. 'That doesn't mean you didn't intend to!'

He took her empty cup, his gaze narrowed on her face yet coolly distant. 'Wait for me while I rinse this and put it away.'

Her eyes dark with misery, Julia watched him disappearing in the dim regions of the house. He wasn't leaving any evidence that she had been here, nor did he intend answering more questions about Lorraine. Helplessly she bowed her head, feeling so devastated she couldn't think straight. Not even his incredible proposal had any reality. She seemed to have made a terrible mess of things. Painfully she swallowed another flood of tears. What was the use of telling herself that repeatedly? She must start concentrating on how to get out of the fix she was in—instead of how she got into it. For everyone's sake!

As the truck sped back through the darkness on the return journey, she soon discovered there was going to be no way out. Guy was adamant that she should marry him. So far as he was concerned, she had played one too many foolish games and must be prepared to suffer the consequences. He drove with such complete detachment that she wondered how such iron control had ever cracked, as it had this evening. It just didn't seem possible.

He took care to see she was sitting comfortably in the front beside him. His glance had silenced her when she had suggested travelling in the back again.

'Sackcloth and ashes isn't really your style, *ma chérie*,' he had said harshly. 'I know what you are, so you don't have to try and impress me.'

'I never have,' she whispered unhappily.

'Only André.'

He still believed, she could tell, that she had come to l'Ejienne to be with André—and what could she say?

'Do you care for him?' His mouth had a cruel twist.

She sensed a catch somewhere. She felt wary without knowing why. 'I don't love him, if that's what you mean.'

'Yet you were going to him, committing yourself.'

Guy's voice was so icy it seemed to freeze her so that she was unable to think clearly. 'C-committing myself?'

'In the eyes of everyone else.'

'Oh, I see.' She stared blindly at the road ahead. His contempt was obvious and she would have earned it if what he believed had been true—that she had been going to André merely for excitement, adventure, without loving him. If only the true story of her intentions had been more palatable! Yet perhaps the moment had come to confess. Guy would be disgusted, surprised, but he mightn't feel it necessary to marry her.

'Guy . . .' she began hoarsely, 'I wasn't—wasn't going . . .'

He stopped her abruptly, his eyes glittering as he briefly turned to her. 'Julia, *s'il te plaît*! I don't want to hear any more. We are going to be married, and I would rather not listen to any prefabrication of stories you are about to think up. You are like many others, I imagine—a moral coward when it comes to a showdown and things aren't going your way.'

'But this involves you,' desperately she tried to get through to him. 'You don't have to be saddled with a wife you don't even like.'

'Stop jumping to the wrong conclusions.'

How could she think otherwise when he looked at her

with hate in his eyes? 'Why should you marry me?' she persisted.

'Why? Perhaps,' his voice was coolly insolent, 'I want more of what I've already had a taste of.'

She couldn't believe that, but, as she shrank instinctively from him, he seemed fleetingly amused by her sharply drawn breath. 'You're trying to shock me,' she whispered hoarsely.

The flicker she had seen in his eyes was cynicism, not amusement, she realised as he asked grimly, 'Would that be possible?'

Julia didn't reply. In his present mood of harsh anger she was afraid to argue with him. He had his mind made up about her and nothing she said was going to make any difference. He had certain codes and lived by them, he wasn't going to allow one foolish young English girl to change his way of thinking. He was concentrating on his driving and judging from the hardness of his face his thoughts were far from pleasant, but he seemed content to leave her alone with her own.

At last she sighed despairingly, 'I know you're refusing to talk about it, but I hope you're going to give yourself time to reconsider. Marriage is a serious undertaking, especially in France, and once you've told Aunt Mavis and made an announcement it might be too late to change your mind.'

'I won't change it, nor do I wish to.' Guy spoke with such finality that she subsided, defeated. When he suggested she should try and get some sleep, she closed her eyes so he wouldn't see the tears in them.

He didn't love her, yet because of what had happened he was prepared to sacrifice all his chances of future happiness. All along he had been protective, something she had come to take for granted, while not realising just how far such a sense of responsibility might take him. Julia didn't think she would ever forgive herself for overlooking this factor when she had gone to l'Ejienne this evening. Having planned so foolishly and impulsively, she was now trapped, and Guy had every right to believe she had trapped him. That her good intentions had failed miserably was no one's fault but her own, and it seemed she must be prepared to pay dearly.

She refused to dwell on what their marriage might be like, aware that she would hope until the last moment it would never take place. A few hours ago the thought of marrying Guy would have filled her with delight, but to be plunged from a naïve girl's vague idea of marital bliss into cold reality had stunned her. The passionate stirrings she had felt in her body, on previous occasions when Guy had kissed her, had been alarming but not unpleasant. What she hadn't realised was the deception of it. The longing and response a man aroused in a girl was really a means to an end, a way of persuading her to allow him to do what he liked with her. Julia admitted unhappily that she hadn't taken her own vulnerability, nor Guy's expertise into account, but if this helped her another time to resist him, then she must have learned a valuable lesson.

Before reaching Champonale, she again asked him if he wouldn't change his mind over marrying her, but he refused to listen. He didn't appear to have wasted the silent hours of their journey in fruitless self-recrimination, as she had, but had everything worked out. His cold-blooded planning Julia found hard to forgive, when she wouldn't have been capable of planning a single thing. It amazed her, too, how no one seemed to question his smooth story about suddenly discovering he was too fond of Julia to wait. Even his brief reference to snatching her from the Renauds' party was swallowed without suspicion when they arrived.

Their wedding, nevertheless, once the news of it leaked out, didn't receive quite such a negative reception, but she was cushioned from the worst of it at l'Ejienne. It was from Monique, who talked incessantly, that Julia learnt how her marriage to Guy was the talk of Provençe and had made headlines even farther afield. That alarmed her, as she hadn't realised the Guerard family were so well known, and it seemed yet another reason to regret not having made a greater effort to remove herself from Guy's life completely.

She had tried. Until the very last moment she had begged Guy to think again. On the eve of their wedding she had even managed to make him listen while she had told him the truth, but he had merely laughed in her face.

'You aren't asking me to believe you would have found the courage to go to my bed and stay there until you were discovered?' he exclaimed, his handsome mouth curling contemptuously at the corners. 'Sometimes I do not take a lot of persuading, but I would never believe that!'

As she had gazed at him with an increasing sense of frustration, Julia had doubted herself if she would ever have found the nerve to get into his bed. 'It was only so you would let me go.'

He had laughed outright at that. 'Many, *ma chérie*, would question your reason, not your reasons.'

The quick anger she had felt at his derision, enabled her to retort, 'If you question yours, in the weeks to come, then don't blame me!'

His anger had been just as swift but disguised. 'You can be sure that I always know what I am doing, Julia. Unlike you, I never act impulsively. We will be married tomorrow, *ma petite*, whether you like it or not. You have proved by your recent behaviour that you require looking after, while I need a wife. And as we are both connected through members of the same family, if not by blood, I consider it a very suitable arrangement, *mignonne*.'

He had assured Julia their wedding would be quiet, but she hadn't thought it would be as quiet as it was. After a brief civil ceremony at the local Mairie, they went alone to the church, with only two close professional friends of Guy's for witnesses, who didn't come to the reception. They didn't have a reception, as such. Mavis and Hortense arranged a light buffet while Guy produced some bottles of champagne which he had purchased some time ago from the Montagne de Rheims, one of the principal grape-producing districts of Champagne, where the sparkling wine was made. There was only Mavis and the staff to drink their health and wish them well, and though Julia trembled throughout, Guy never appeared to be disturbed for a moment.

Julia, following Guy's implicit instructions, did her best to look happy. She wasn't sure if her frequent attempts to smile were always successful, but no one seemed surprised that she wasn't completely composed. Pretending to be a radiant bride was a greater strain than she had imagined, and although she had been dreading it, she was relieved when the time came for them to leave.

Mavis, she suspected, was having as much trouble as she was keeping a smile pinned to her face. Guy, she knew, had given his stepmother only a brief explanation regarding his sudden decision to marry, but Mavis didn't appear to doubt he had snatched Julia from her friend's party to make a dawn proposal. Cleverly, Julia thought, he had asked Mavis to contact l'Ejienne for him, to make sure everything was prepared, knowing that Monique would confirm that he had been there alone.

But despite her apparent acceptance of the situation, Julia couldn't help feeling that, underneath, Mavis was hurt. She had looked forward to Guy's wedding for so long it would have been impossible for her to feel otherwise at the way things had been rushed. And, instead of Lorraine being the beautiful bride, it was her young niece from London, who, though her sister's child, she might consider entirely unsuitable for such a position. That she had made little reference to the wedding in the days leading up to it, seemed to confirm this, and for Julia had added fresh undercurrents to an atmosphere already becoming rapidly unbearable.

Observing Mavis's uneasiness, Julia hated herself for being responsible. Her aunt loved her, she was sure, but she wondered if she still would when the truth came out. That it could be kept from her for ever, Julia found impossible to believe. Perhaps the full story would never be revealed, but how could two people pretend to be happily married when they were not? Soon Mavis must begin to notice something was badly wrong, and Julia despaired to think of the effect it might have on her.

They left for l'Ejienne scarcely two hours after being married.

'No sense in prolonging something no one was enjoying,' Guy remarked with brutal frankness as they waved goodbye.

'Aunt Mavis is naturally bewildered,' Julia retorted stiffly, 'but she has been, since the beginning.'

'The rush was unavoidable, but she'll soon come round.'

So he had noticed Mavis wasn't merely upset by the usual wedding nerves. She might have known, because he never missed a thing—it was his indifference that made her angry. 'It might have helped if you'd allowed her to tell Fayme.'

'I'm a monster already because of what you believe I've done to you,' he shrugged. 'You can't think worse of me because I preferred to keep my sister away from my wedding.'

'But that's just it!' Julia cried. 'She is your sister, and she's likely to blame me!'

'She knows me too well to do that,' he returned mildly. 'She won't question that it was my decision.'

Julia fumed. 'That won't stop her, like me, wondering why!'

'I didn't think you would need to ask,' Guy said blandly. 'If Fayme had known, so would half the country, and if you fancied Léon turning up with his camera crews accompanied by the press, I didn't.'

'The truth's more probably that you're ashamed of me!' Julia exclaimed fiercely.

'The truth is,' he corrected harshly, 'I was trying to save you unnecessary distress. Do you think I would have cared if all the media in the world had been there, you little fool!'

She deserved that, Julia acknowledged, bowing her fair head, murmuring an apology. She wasn't sure where the fierce desire to fight him was coming from. It was as though something inside her was building up and seeking frantically for a kind of violent release. During the past few days she had rarely been alone with Guy and when she had he had had little to say to her, but she still felt scorched by feelings she couldn't explain.

For all her brief remorse, she felt anger flare again as she heard him say coolly, 'When our son is married, we must see it is a traditional affair, then I might be forgiven.'

His coolness was like a barricade, a door he kept firmly closed against all her hopes and fears. Talking of sons must be an extra taunt as she was sure he wouldn't intend having any, not as long as he was married to her, anyway. 'There's just no getting through to you, is there?' she cried, using derision to cover a sudden sense of grief.

'What do you think you've been doing ever since you came here?' he snapped, but so enigmatically, she was silenced.

Dropping back in her seat, she closed her eyes, pretending his comment wasn't worthy of a reply. It could mean all sorts of things, but most probably he was hinting she was a problem he hadn't been able to ignore and could well have done without. Having her eyes shut also prevented her from looking at him. Once her glance rested on his dark features, his lean jaw and hard but sensuous mouth, she found it difficult to look away. Today, in the twelfth-century grey stone church where they were married, he had seemed formidable. Big, dark and powerful, he had towered by her side, holding her hand firmly in long, finely made fingers which had gripped with a hurtful strength. She had looked at him once, until a shiver had run down her spine and her heavy lashes had fallen helplessly. He hadn't kissed her after the ceremony, but even in church a feeling of sexual tension had lain between them. Despairingly, Julia wondered why it was always there. It was something she didn't understand but was as potent as kisses.

'Will Bernard and Monique be expecting us?' She was forced to speak in order to steady her racing pulse.

'Yes,' he replied, not rebuking her for asking a question to which she already knew the answer.

Try as she might, Julia couldn't decide what Monique was going to make of Guy getting married so quickly. No one drove the distance he had a few nights ago to stay only an hour or two and then leave. Especially when he had arranged to stay! A man in love might, but Monique, if she was any kind of woman at all, was going to take one look at Guy's sombre face and begin to wonder.

Following on her thoughts, Julia observed bitterly. 'Perhaps you should tell me how we're going to make people believe we're a normal married couple?'

'By being one.'

Julia clenched her hands. 'I'm sorry, I don't understand.'

He smiled, not sympathetically. 'It won't be too difficult, if you co-operate.'

Her heart thudded; she couldn't even consider this. 'I've never been much good at pretending,' she replied swiftly, forgetting she had been doing just that for weeks. Remembering, she winced. She loved Guy and she must spend the rest of her life pretending she didn't.

'You were going to be an actress,' he reminded her dryly.

'That was just a crazy idea.'

'But you would have tried.' His mouth twisted, as if he recalled how long it had taken him to talk her out of it. 'I suggest if you apply the same determination to our marriage, *ma chérie*, you won't go far wrong.'

Bernard was waiting for them, as he had been the last time they had arrived. As Guy helped Julia from the truck, which he had brought instead of a car, as it was still loaded with urgently needed supplies, she felt Bernard regarding her curiously. She was so cramped from sitting so long that she was glad of Guy's assistance, and the sense of reassurance it somehow gave.

Being able to see Bernard, as she hadn't been on that other occasion, she was pleasantly surprised to find him younger than Guy, which could mean his wife might be nearer her own age.

As Guy introduced them she liked the quick warmth in Bernard's face, the impression it somehow left that he liked her and wouldn't be unduly critical. Monique was the same. When Bernard went with them to the house and his wife came running from the direction of the kitchens, where, Julia recalled, Guy had taken her empty cup, she was relieved to see, as she had hoped, that Monique could be no more than thirty and looked really pleased to see her. She was young and very pretty, and she and Bernard obviously adored each other.

'Welcome to l'Ejienne,' she said, her warm smile swiftly masking a hint of astonishment. If she was clearly startled by Julia's delicate fairness, she only allowed it to show for a moment. 'Bernard and I won't pretend we weren't puzzled to find your note, Guy,' she nodded towards the hall table, 'but when Madame rang today, after lunch and explained, we understood. We hope you will both be very happy.'

She kissed Guy resoundingly on either cheek and, more uncertainly, shook hands with Julia, then, after telling them their dinner was all prepared and waiting, she grasped Bernard's hand and dragged him away. Over her shoulder she said something very quickly to Guy in French, which Julia failed to catch.

'What did she say?' As the door closed behind them, Julia frowned warily.

'Ah,' briefly Monique's teasing laughter was echoed in his eyes, 'she was congratulating me, *ma mie*, on my beautiful bride.'

It had all taken place so quickly—their arrival, meeting the Laportes, that Julia felt dazed. Monique was a good-looking girl, well dressed and discreetly made up. Even so, she had left the mark of her lipstick on Guy's cheek, and Julia's glance rested on it doubtfully.

Guy rubbed a finger over it and it came away red. 'At least Monique shows the right kind of enthusiasm,' he mocked harshly.

Julia's neck became as colourful as his finger. 'Didn't she say something about dinner?' she queried tentatively, changing the subject, but not because she was hungry.

While his glance revealed all too clearly that he considered her a coward, he didn't tease her any more. 'Mavis must have left instructions. Shall we go and see?'

He led the way to a large kitchen with walls and fireplace made of red stone. Julia liked it at once. She was growing used to French kitchens being much more attractive than the average English ones, but there was something rather special about this one. The tables and chairs were in a simple country style and she loved the honey-coloured wood. Her eyes wandered to the many shelves, laden with baskets and bottles, local ceramic pottery and peasant wares. She loved the smells, too, the faint aroma of herbs mingling with the more pungent ones from strings of onions and newly baked bread along with the appetising hint of something cooking—she guessed, their dinner.

After inspecting various dishes. Guy turned to her. 'There's nothing that can't wait, if you'd like to shower first.'

'No,' she moved towards the stone sink in a corner, 'I'll just wash my hands.'

The table was set. In the middle stood a lovely blue, cast-iron casserole full of *bouillabaisse* a delicious soup that they art with some equally delicious onion caraway bread. Then, from the oven, Guy carved thin slices of succulent lamb which he served with dauphinoise potatoes and a few other vegetables. With this they drank a bottle of Chateau Léoville Las-Cases, a wonderful claret which tasted so lovely, Julia drank more than she would have done ordinarily.

Throughout the meal, Guy watched her broodingly, a slightly unpleasant curve to his mouth which Julia concluded could only have to do with her, because the food was first class. At one time, on raising her heavy, wine-sleepy eyes to his dark face, she wondered vaguely if he was enjoying what he was eating, or if he even realised he was eating anything at all. He looked tired, she thought, with a surge of pity that was entirely new to her. It was a feeling of compassion, of wanting to care for him and sacrifice everything, as he had done for her. It was the firmer foundations on which an enduring love might be built, and she trembled as she recognised the depth of her own commitment.

When she refused the sweet and coffee, Guy rose to his feet, saying he would see her to her room. 'You are falling asleep in your chair,' he rasped curtly. 'There are more comfortable places.'

'My—room?' her eyes widened uncertainly, beautiful cloudy pools.

'Yes.' His voice was cold as he tore his glance from her face. 'You are next to me. Mavis is of the belief that the English prefer separate rooms. She ordered

Monique to prepare them, but it is up to us which we use.'

Julia didn't reply; she was at a loss how to. A flush stained her cheeks while her rapidly beating heart made coherent thought impossible. If Guy had given one sign she suspected she would have thrown herself into his arms, but he looked so forbidding that the inclination died almost before it was born.

Stumbling behind him into her room, as he flung open the door, she gazed at it doubtfully, her mind telling her one thing, her body another. The bed wasn't turned down and with an impatient mutter, he went to do it for her. Julia stared at the play of muscles in his powerful arms and thighs as he bent to perform the simple task. Monique must have been far from sure they would sleep separately, she realised suddenly; she hadn't just carelessly overlooked one of her duties, as Guy's impatience seemed to imply.

Conscious that inside she was full of strange yearnings which were objecting to being denied, she closed her eyes helplessly and swayed towards him as he returned to her.

'You're nearly out on your feet!' he said roughly, picking her up and laying her on the bed.

Julia, her heart now racing madly, believed he must mean to kiss her. When he began to straighten it was more than she could endure. 'Guy!' she moaned, her arms rising to stop him, the plea on her lips incomprehensible but her meaning clear.

He paused, his eyes narrowed, as if he couldn't believe her silent invitation. 'Yes?' he breathed curtly.

When it came to it, she found she was still too shy to beg shamelessly for something he didn't want to give. 'Are—aren't you going to kiss me goodnight?' was the best she could manage, and even this made her feel totally humiliated.

Yet when he gathered her in his arms and his hard mouth found hers, she didn't resist him. She gave herself up to him and didn't try and control the hot flame that suddenly burst like a furnace inside her. She wanted him desperately, she was only just realising how much, and because they were married she saw no need to suppress her feelings. Yet at the same time she was aware of the same deep panicky virginal instinct to escape from him that she had known before.

The hand that had been pushing his shirt open tensed against the mat of dark hair, but Guy's urgency didn't give her a chance to consider such contradictory feelings. His kiss became passionate in its intensity as he appeared to take her co-operation for granted, and his body descended heavily on hers. She felt the uneven thud of his heart accelerate under her fingers and his arm tighten on her waist as sudden tremors of response began shooting right through her. As her lips parted, his mouth probed deeply, while roughly and sensuously his hands began caressing her.

Julia trembled as they clung together as though seared by some electric force. A low sound came from Guy's throat and his arms were like a vice, crushing her slenderness to him. She could feel her breasts hurting against the hard wall of his chest and his lips were suddenly hot and demanding. Involuntarily she arched against him, longing to be even closer, their clothing becoming an insufferable barrier.

'Guy!' Desire rose so fiercely it made her voice sharp. She didn't realise her gasping exclamation sounded more like a frantic appeal.

He paused, raising himself sufficiently to let the air cool his skin, which immediately appeared to bring a return to sanity. With a growl of disgust he was off the bed, on his feet, before she could collect her lost senses.

'I'm sorry, Julia,' he said tightly, completely misunderstanding her reactions. 'The first time I hurt you, and I vowed it wouldn't happen again.'

'It was my fault,' Julia whispered hoarsely.

'Yes, you're a little slut,' he agreed grimly, 'though that doesn't absolve me completely. You have to remember that a man is easily aroused—even when his feelings aren't involved. When they are it can be even more dangerous.'

CHAPTER TEN

As the door closed behind him, Julia took her hands from her burning face to stare at it. It was solid and plain, but on it she seemed to see clearly the imprint of his powerful body. His tall, broad-shouldered figure danced crazily before her eyes and only pride kept her from running after him. His last sentence would have been enough to stop someone far less sensitive than herself, she thought miserably.

Licking her bruised lips, seeking unconsciously to ease the pain inflicted by his mouth, she knew she wanted him desperately, and it must have shown. Humiliation added more colour to her cheeks as she dropped her head to her bent knees. Guy had guessed she would be content to belong to him, even realising he didn't love her. Now he would only despise her, probably more than he had done before.

Her eyes hot and dry, she set about preparing for bed, but although the shower was refreshing it failed to provide the solution she was searching for. How to arm herself against the temptation of a man who had been her husband for less than twelve hours? The first time Guy had made love to her, and again this evening, she had found herself reaching towards something she hadn't been able to see. It had been shrouded in mystery. What she did know instinctively was that she would never be content until she discovered what it was.

Guy was out next morning when she went down for breakfast, and despite some relief she was aware of a flicker of disappointment. It was Monique who greeted her as she walked into the kitchen and smiled sympathetically as she saw Julia's face fall.

169

'Already you miss him very much, *mademoiselle*?' she said softly, before exclaiming, 'Oh, I'm sorry. I should have said *madame*, but you look so young.'

Julia smiled back. 'Why bother with either? My name's Julia.'

Monique's eyes warmed with appreciation as she whisked a coffee pot off the stove. 'I was just about to bring you some coffee, so it is ready.'

Julia obediently sat down as Monique waved a hand towards the table and began pouring the steaming liquid into two cups. 'You don't mind if I join you?'

'Of course not!' Julia laughed. 'But I don't want you spoiling me.'

'All brides should be spoiled a little.' Monique studied Julia, appraising the light cotton dress she wore. 'Guy went out with Bernard after breakfast.'

'I should have been up to get it.' Julia immediately felt guilty.

'Why should you?' Monique exclaimed quickly. 'I'm here, and that is what I get paid for.'

Somehow Julia couldn't believe Monique was just an ordinary servant. Biting into a warm roll, liberally spread with the most wonderful cherry jam, she waited a moment before asking carefully, 'Have you and your husband worked for Guy long?'

'We have been here almost ten years.' Monique appeared to welcome the query, rather than resent it. 'Bernard learned viticulture at a leading university. I was there studying something else, but that is how we met. Bernard's father is a famous *marchand de vin* in Paris, and Guy's good friend. That is why, when Bernard confessed he was more interested in growing grapes than marketing the wine, Guy offered him a job at l'Ejienne.'

'Didn't you want a career?'

'But I have one!' Monique laughed, 'as Bernard's wife, the mother of his children. We love living here almost as much as we love each other. In other words,' she lifted expressive shoulders, 'I am disgracefully content!'

After they finished their coffee, she showed Julia round the house. 'A lot of it is closed up, as you can see, for Guy is seldom here apart from the *vendange*, in September. I did intend opening some of the downstairs rooms, as you can't live in the kitchen.'

'You must let me help,' Julia said eagerly.

Monique glanced at her doubtfully. 'But you are on your honeymoon!'

Julia forced herself to joke about it. 'And already deserted by my husband.'

'No,' Monique smiled but sounded very emphatic, 'that I do not believe. It is merely that you were married in a hurry at a time when he has much to do. In another day or so, when he is through, he will devote himself to you completely. And,' she added, her eyes twinkling but faintly wistful, 'there are few women in the Rhone Valley who will not envy you, *ma chère*.'

Guy didn't return until it was time for lunch, and before then Monique had to leave as one of her children had been sent home from school, unwell. A worker from the estate came to seek her, and to set her mind at rest Julia assured her that she could manage for the rest of the day. As Monique had already made a fresh batch of bread, Julia merely put out some cold meats and salads and sat down to wait.

When Guy came, his eyes swept her pale face, but he made no comment other than that he wasn't very hungry.

'I haven't done a lot,' Julia said awkwardly, with a sense of frustration as she met his cool gaze. 'Monique has been here all morning, but her little boy is ill and she had to leave.'

'We'll go out this evening.' He left the sink, to dry his hands on a rough white towel. 'It will save you the bother of cooking, and Monique should be back tomorrow.'

'Oh, I don't mind.' She averted her eyes from the virile strength of his body in his tight-fitting pants and open-necked shirt. Trembling, she plugged in the percolater. They were like strangers, she thought despondently. If it hadn't been for the almost visible tension between them it would be easy to believe they were two people meeting for the first time.

Guy ate the meat from the night before and some locally cured dried beef washed down with red wine from his own cellar.

Julia refused more than a small glass of it, ruefully observing that she hadn't the head for it. 'I drank too much last night.'

Whether or not he thought she was hinting that this had been responsible for her feverish response to his kisses, she had no idea. He merely smiled thinly and said, 'Rhone wines are very alcoholic and really need food to go with them. For parties and drinking on their own, it's better to choose something lighter.'

She wanted to ask him about Rhone wines, how the grapes were grown, the wine made. It was all new to her and she felt an urge to learn, but she suspected Guy had no inclination to teach her. He was merely talking to take some of the strain from the atmosphere.

He drained his coffee cup and stood up. 'I have to go out again this afternoon, I'm afraid.'

'Are you very busy?' She drew a deep breath. 'Can't I help?' Her cheeks flushed when he looked faintly amused and shook his head. 'Everyone,' she retorted, 'has to learn.'

'Julia,' he said curtly, 'this is a big property and each time I come there are decisions to be made. It's not possible to leave everything to Bernard, but there's nothing you can do.'

'In September, when you pick the grapes,' she insisted stubbornly, 'you must need extra help.'

'We'll see.' His mouth tightened, as if her insistence irritated him. Without looking at her he prepared to leave. 'Make yourself beautiful for this evening,' he shrugged.

He spoke so absently she couldn't believe he cared and in a fit of resentment spent the afternoon cleaning the drawing-room, hoping the hard work would make her look so worn out he wouldn't want to take her anywhere.

Monique popped in just as she was finishing, and threw up her hands in a mixture of admiration and dismay as she saw the room restored to something of its former glory. 'What is Guy going to say?' she exclaimed, rolling her eyes heavenward, but somehow she seemed more interested in what she had to say herself. 'The newspapers are full of your wedding, Julia. I didn't bring one for you to read as I wasn't sure Guy would approve.'

Julia's eyes widened unhappily. 'What's in them?'

'Nothing to worry about,' Monique replied hastily. 'Just a lot of silly tittle-tattle and conjecture which would only bore you. I only came to tell you for fear you heard of it unexpectedly from another source and were upset. You know what men are. Guy might think he was protecting you by keeping it from you.'

When Monique had departed, after Julia had thanked her for coming and enquired after her son, the phone rang. As there was no one else in, Julia answered and was startled to hear Lorraine speaking.

'Is Guy there?' she asked sharply.

'No . . .'

'It doesn't matter.' Lorraine, appearing to anticipate what Julia had been going to suggest, didn't let her go on. 'You needn't fetch him. It's you I want to talk to.'

Instinct urged Julia to hang up. Later she wished she had, but her overriding feelings were of guilt, so she ignored the small, warning voice inside her. If she owed Lorraine nothing else, it must be a hearing. Hadn't she told Julia many times how she and Guy were to be married? By putting him in a position where he had felt forced to marry the wrong girl, Julia knew she must have ruined two lives.

In Lorraine's furious reproaches, there was nothing she hadn't heard before, but there was one item which succeeded in making her feel worse than she did already.

'I don't know how you got Guy up the aisle,' Lorraine sneered insolently. 'It was such a rushed affair that everyone is jumping to the same conclusions.'

'They're—wrong!'

'Can't you speak up instead of whispering?' Lorraine exclaimed. 'I warned Guy, when he told me he had promised your father he would look after you, to watch out. But it seems even the wariest can be cleverly trapped. Nevertheless, he means to divorce you.'

Julia wasn't sure when the receiver dropped from her nerveless hand and Lorraine's venomous voice stopped abusing her numb ears. Lorraine must have seen the newspaper reports of the wedding, unless Fayme had been in touch with her, which was quite possible as Guy had given Mavis permission to ring Fayme as soon as they left, yesterday.

Her eyes aching with unshed tears, Julia wondered how her father could have done such a thing. It explained so much, especially why Guy had felt honour-bound to marry her. But for her father's request he might have let her go, even after making love to her.

It amazed Julia how, after all this, after she had showered and dressed, she only looked slightly pale. Make-up helped, she supposed, unaware that it didn't conceal the hint of desperation in her eyes. Guy hadn't told her what to wear, so she had chosen at random a silky gold dress, belted tightly at her waist and flaring out to just below her knee, the most popular length, she had discovered, for all but the most formal occasions. The bodice plunged, perhaps rather too deeply, and the gold might have looked a bit spectacular with her hair, but she was too preoccupied with other things to care.

'Where are we going?' she asked absently, as they left the house some time later, after Guy had returned and changed.

'Wait and see,' he replied curtly.

She was quite prepared to. It didn't seem to matter where they went or how long it took to get there. She was still trying to decide the best way to approach him regarding her father. Because she felt more like attacking him than mentioning the matter quietly, she tried to wait until she could be reasonably sure of keeping her temper before she spoke.

When, after an hour, she failed to find sufficient composure, she began hoping he might give her a lead, perhaps by making some remark about their marriage, but he said nothing. There was only the taut, now familiar silence between them, which, with every mile, became more impossible to break.

Guy, in a dark jacket and tie, which enhanced the formidable width of his shoulders and lent an autocratic air to his dark head, seemed more unapproachable as the miles sped by. She was aware they had crossed the Rhone, but as darkness fell she had no idea where they were. When they drew up, at last, outside a house, from which sounds of music and laughter reached them, she was startled.

Bewildered and somehow apprehensive, she turned to her husband. 'Where are we?'

'At a friend's,' he replied smoothly, his eyes slanting expressionlessly to her anxious face. 'They're giving a party to which we're invited. You didn't imagine I was gate-crashing, did you?'

'But you didn't say!'

'Aren't I allowed to surprise you?' he quipped coldly. 'Anyway, I thought it might be more fun than sitting staring vacantly at each other over a restaurant table.'

Something about him seemed to suggest that if her mood had been angry, his verged on violence, but Julia put this aside as being fanciful. 'Won't they think it strange? I mean,' she faltered miserably, her cheeks hot, 'we are supposed to be on our honeymoon.'

'The press appear to think so too,' he muttered sourly.

So he knew—and had let her sit in tormented silence! 'Sometimes I hate you!' she whispered.

'Shall we see?' he retorted harshly, and didn't seem disturbed when she didn't understand what he meant.

Somehow, Julia felt terrible about coming here. Her nerves screaming, she hung back, and because of this provided Guy with an easy excuse for almost dragging her inside. A more comprehensive glance told her it was a property something like the one Guy owned on the other side of the Rhone, and suddenly she was struck by a frightening sense of enlightenment.

'Who lives here?' she gasped, as she was urged none too gently towards a middle-aged couple.

'Don't you realise?' he quipped, moments before he introduced her to their hosts, Monsieur and Madame Tissier.

'My wife,' he presented her suavely.

'Why, Guy!' they were clearly surprised but delighted, 'We sent word, because we thought Bernard and Monique might come. We felt it was too much to hope for that you would.'

'I thought we might drop in for a few minutes,' Guy smiled, 'You've been away a long time.'

Why did she feel he had come here tonight, more as a kind of experiment. 'They're André's parents!' Julia choked, almost in horror, as, with an adroitness she was coming to recognise, Guy whisked her away before she could meet anyone else.

'I wondered when you would realise,' he snapped. 'And here comes the great man himself.'

It seemed like a nightmare that it wasn't only André who confronted her but also Lorraine. If she failed to comprehend how Lorraine could be here after talking to her on the phone not long ago, Julia soon found out.

'I came this morning,' Lorraine sidled up to Guy, taking hold of his arm as she explained. 'Fayme couldn't make it and begged me to come instead. Your sister has suffered greatly because of your marriage, Guy,' she pouted.

'I don't imagine she will suffer long,' Guy replied coldly, meeting Lorraine's eyes.

Julia felt anger and misery flood through her. Despite the coldness of his manner, she was convinced he couldn't have assured Lorraine more clearly that his marriage was merely a temporary one. When André, appearing to find his voice at last, asked Guy's permission—which was given—to dance with the bride, she had never felt so unhappy in her life.

Guy must have been pleased to get rid of her as Julia noticed he immediately began dancing with Lorraine. Her defeated eyes, following their progress, watched helplessly as he steered his partner over the room to a door that led to the gardens. She was so stunned by this she failed to realise that André had manoeuvred her outside as well but in the opposite direction.

As he paused in a shadowy recess of the terrace, she glanced at him in alarmed indignation. She had no desire to be alone with André, and how could she criticise Guy for going off with Lorraine if she was guilty of a similar crime herself?

'I'd like to go back,' she said quickly. 'Please, André!'

'In a moment,' he said tersely, letting go of her but keeping one hand on her arm. 'When you've told me why you did it, Julia.'

'You mean, why did I marry Guy?'

'Yes.'

She didn't feel angry. Because André had asked her to marry him, she believed he had a right to ask why she had chosen another man. There was an answer but she was reluctant to voice it as this would be the first time she had said it aloud. Yet when it fell from her lips she was unable to stop it. 'I love him, André.'

'I thought as much,' he muttered bleakly, his face pale but resigned, as if it was something he had suspected for a while. 'All the same, it is a shock to hear you confirm it,' he said hoarsely, 'and if I didn't care for you so much, I should have found it impossible to forgive you.'

'I'm sorry,' she whispered, she felt inadequately.

He smiled faintly. 'So am I, *ma mie*, but against Guy I could never hope to win.'

If only he knew the whole truth! Julia bit her lip sharply as she turned to go inside again. She had no wish to stay with André any longer, for fear of revealing something which was better left unsaid.

André, though, begged her to remain. 'The happy bride and the rejected suitor.' His eyes lightened whimsically. 'We must make an odd pair! Come and have one last drink with me, *ma petite*, then you can leave me to drown my sorrows alone.'

How could she refuse? Besides, Guy was nowhere to be seen and she had no wish to go searching for him and perhaps find him with Lorraine in his arms. A light buffet complete with drinks had been set out on the moonlit lawns as well as in the house, and she allowed André to guide her towards it.

The grounds were extensive and more elaborate than those at l'Ejienne, but when she commented on this André merely said that Guy could do a lot more there if he wanted to. He seemed disinclined to make comparisons, and Julia felt she had been tactless.

There was a crowd round the buffet which was arranged on the paved area beside the swimming pool. The people goodhumouredly fighting for food were mostly young. Julia was thankful that she couldn't see a familiar face and that no one appeared to connect her with the girl Guy Guerard had married.

Even so, she was relieved when André suggested she

waited by the pool while he fetched their drinks. It was incredible, just as he was turning away, that two young men, joking boisterously if innocently with each other, should catch her inadvertently and knock her into it.

As Julia sank under the water, at the deep end, she heard cries of alarm. Then André dived in, pulling her out, whipping her up in his arms as she choked and her legs crumpled under her. Not many people had seen what had happened, and the few who had, he brushed aside, along with the two remorseful boys as he carried Julia back to the house.

He went in by a side door. It was over so quickly, Julia didn't quite realise what had happened until she found herself being dropped gently on André's bed. Hitting the water at an awkward angle seemed briefly to have stunned her and for a few moments she scarcely knew where she was.

'I'm sorry, *ma mie*!' André, clearly in some state of shock himself, was babbling. 'Speak to me! Tell me you are all right!' As she gulped and nodded, he began tearing off her wet dress. 'I'll bring you something else to wear.' He averted his eyes quickly from her near-naked body and stumbled in the direction of a closet.

'I—I shouldn't be here!' Julia gasped, trying belatedly to cover herself, wondering frantically what she was going to do about her dress.

André searching distractedly through his wardrobe, sounded indistinct. 'I couldn't leave you down there! For one thing, Guy wouldn't have thanked me, not after all the publicity in the papers today. It would only have been moments before someone recognised you, and then the fat would have been in the fire!'

Julia couldn't argue against such logic, she was still too dazed. Her hair seemed to have suffered no ill affects. She was wearing it tightly coiled about her small head and the water hadn't had time to penetrate. If André could put her dress in a tumbler-drier she might be able to go downstairs again in a few minutes.

She suggested this after wrapping herself tightly in the bathrobe he brought her, and he agreed. It was unfortunate that as he bent to pick up her dress from the floor at her feet, he diverted impulsively to kiss her, and in the same instant, the door crashed open and Guy strode in.

His voice was like a minor explosion, smashing into them sideways. '*Mon Dieu*—what the hell's going on!'

'Wait a minute!' André involuntarily flung a protective arm around Julia's shoulders. 'I don't know what's on your mind . . .'

It looked like murder, if the darkness of Guy's face was anything to go by. Julia struggled to her feet with a strangled cry. 'I was coming down . . .'

'After—what?'

'Take it easy!' André intervened hotly. 'You're going too far.'

'Not as far as you'd go if I had more time.' Guy advanced while André stepped back warily.

Guy's anger was knife-edged. Like André, Julia retreated, falling back on the bed, which seemed to incense him further. Viciously he swept her from it, carrying her to his car. He must have known the house fairly well for he never faltered. He went out through a rear entrance and, as they had been some of the last to arrive, there was no other vehicle in the way to prevent them leaving almost immediately.

Julia, crushed by the fierceness of his arms and still chilled from the pool, was feeling very fragile. The force he had used to thrust her into the car hadn't helped either.

'Guy?' she whispered, sudden tears in her eyes.

No answer.

'Won't you listen?' she begged. It took a lot of nerve to speak at all, for she had never seen him so furious.

'Shut up!'

'I . . .' she made another attempt.

'If you say one more word,' he snarled, 'so help me, I might kill you!'

She couldn't remember a journey being as long. Her damp underthings dried but felt sticky and uncomfortable, and while André's bathrobe provided warmth it was a constant reminder of what had happened. What was to happen now? she wondered miserably. Was Guy about to throw her out and terminate their marriage? Perhaps he had every right to be furious, finding her in André's room, but it seemed to Julia that he had been very keen to jump to the wrong conclusions. If he had waited it wouldn't have been difficult to have convinced him he had completely misjudged the situation.

On arriving at l'Ejienne, although the stress of the silent journey had shaken her, Julia was able to walk into the house. Guy's manner was calm, but she could feel his eyes burning into her back as he followed her, and somehow his grim control frightened her.

As he didn't attempt to help, or even touch her, she hoped to escape to her own room, once they were inside, but as she moved towards the stairs, his hands swiftly grasped her, and her nervousness flared to panic as he savagely dragged her to the kitchen.

'Now,' he snapped harshly, 'off with that robe!'

No way was she going to parade in front of him with practically nothing on. 'I will—upstairs!' she protested hoarsely.

He merely smiled, or at least his lips stretched. As though he almost welcomed her defiance, he ripped the offending garment from her shoulders and flung it into the stove. Horrified, Julia watched the flames devouring it hungrily before he closed the door.

'That was André's!' she gasped.

'I'll reimburse him,' he snapped.

Suddenly, with another gasp of horror, realising she was nearly naked, Julia whirled from him, but he caught her up in his arms again.

'You aren't going any more places without me

tonight—or ever,' he said bitterly. 'Perhaps I can discover how far your friend André has violated my rights!'

'He hasn't . . .'

Her protest was cut off by his mouth. He negotiated the stairs swiftly and she didn't get her breath back until they reached his room. Without ceremony he dropped her in the middle of the huge bed and followed. Pulling her roughly into his arms, he turned her face up to meet his, and though she was trembling with fear, she could offer no resistance. He watched her lying there, studying the helpless appeal in her eyes with total indifference, and when the searing possession of his mouth again parted her lips, hot flames shot through her veins, melting her bones and burning her flesh with a feverish heat. She shuddered as he cradled her head at a precise angle, making escape impossible.

Longing shivered through her as his shaking fingers pushed their way under her bra and he began deliberately making love to her. She could hear his breathing quicken, feel his heart pounding in his chest, but some of the terrible anger seemed to leave him. Faintly she recognised that passion was taking them both over, and she tried desperately to temper her own responses so she could find enough strength to push him away.

When he had made love to her before, it had been a fight to the finish and she had wanted the next time to be different. She had wanted Guy to be in love with her, as she was with him, now she knew this could never be. He loved Lorraine, she was the woman he cared for. He was kissing his wife merely as an act of revenge for dragging him from Lorraine and the party, and for attempting to besmirch his good name.

'Guy!' her hands thrust weakly against his disturbed heartbeat. 'Please won't you listen?'

'No.' Having eased from her slightly to throw off his shirt, he completed the action. When the rest of his clothes hit the floor, she gasped.

He crouched over her, his hard maleness more dominant than she had allowed for. Her traitorous senses began swimming as the banked desire in his eyes scorched her helpless limbs. A hand swept over her bare stomach, knocking the breath from her lungs, then his arms were around her, enclosing her fiercely as his hard body descended. She was gathered so tightly to him, she could feel his racing heart exciting her into a kind of mad stampede.

'If I teach you nothing else,' she heard him mutter hoarsely, 'I will teach you how to be a faithful wife!'

Then the telephone rang. There was an extension by the bed and he let it ring. When it didn't stop he swore under his breath and lifted the receiver. 'Yes?' he barked. *'Mon dieu!'* after a second. 'You have a nerve!'

Julia realised it must be André, although she couldn't make out what he was talking about. Her blood ran cold as she noted Guy's returning anger.

While she was weighing her chances of getting through the door before she was caught, she was startled to hear him snap.

'You say she was knocked into the pool and was half unconscious when you got her out. Why didn't you tell me?'

Another pause. 'Yes, I agree, it was my own fault. I wouldn't listen, but I seem to go crazy where Julia is concerned. No, I take your word for it and apologise. I'm very grateful. Now, if you'll excuse me, I have to apologise to Julia as well.'

As he made to end the conversation, André added something more, something which appeared to stun him to complete silence. Julia forgot about running away as she watched a muscle flex in his jaw and heard him exclaim thickly, 'She does?'

Whatever André had said must have had a peculiar effect on him, for he was still looking dazed as he laid down the phone.

'Guy?'

He didn't answer her low-voiced appeal. Instead he removed himself from the bed to shrug into his dressing-gown. Then, his face hard and pale, he pulled a sheet gently up over Julia, covering the nakedness she had somehow completely forgotten about before he sat down again.

Julia found his silence even more frightening than it had been before. 'What did André say to you?' she whispered.

She laid a quick hand on his arm, an unconsciously beseeching gesture. As his glance fell on it, a spasm of pain crossed his face. 'He said you loved me.'

'Oh . . .' Julia lowered her head, feeling wholly shaken. For a brief moment she had feared she was going to hear that André had asserted she loved him, but from relief her mind swung dizzily to anguish. How Guy must be laughing at her! Hurt bred a recklessness she couldn't control. Well, let him have the last laugh— didn't he deserve it? What right had she to feel badly done by?

'He was speaking the truth,' as she spoke she heard Guy's sharply drawn breath but was unable to look at him. 'I've loved you almost from the beginning. It was because I loved you so much that I tried to leave you. I planned to get out of your life, but everything went wrong.'

'Julia!' he attempted to interrupt, but she wouldn't let him.

With tears streaming down her cheeks, she gasped incoherently. 'Instead of leaving you free to marry Lorraine, you were forced to marry me. I'm an encumbrance you're saddled with permanently.'

'Julia!' This time she had to pause, as suddenly he caught her to him with a kind of desperate determination. 'You don't know what you're talking about! I never wanted Lorraine or any other woman, only you. Don't cry, *ma mie*,' he implored huskily, when her tears refused to stop. 'You're the only one I've ever loved—

or wanted to be saddled with permanently,' he added, with a shaken hint of humour.

'But,' Julia's confusion grew, 'how can you speak of loving me when Lorraine rang this afternoon and said you're going to get a divorce?'

'Why didn't you say something?' Guy stared at her white face, his own grim. 'She was making it up.'

Suddenly it didn't seem to matter any more. Her only desire was to remove the strain and despair from his eyes, and, incredibly, it seemed only she could do it. Compulsively she moved against him, feeling his muscles tense as she clung to him, letting him see something of the naked longing in her eyes. 'I love you, Guy,' she whispered, 'I want——' but the rest of her words were lost as his mouth came down fiercely on hers, parting her lips and staking a claim she knew he would never relinquish. Then he was once again lying beside her, his hands making short work of their clothing, and roaming feverishly over her, leaving a trails of fire on her skin.

If the first time had brought little more than pain, now his caresses filled her with ecstatic pleasure. And as they kissed, with mutual, mounting passion, banked-down fires blazed to the heat of a furnace. He kissed her lips and the pink crests of her breasts until her fingers curled convulsively into his thick dark hair to hold him tightly against her. For a brief instant she tried to control a spinning world, but the warmth and light and sensation he was creating within her won and mindlessly she gave herself up to the exquisite frenzy generating between them. Her body yearned for release, but he made her wait, as though he couldn't deny himself one intoxicating moment. He moved to pull her even closer in his arms while his lips tormented her until she cried out in frustration.

'Guy . . .!' she moaned helplessly, and just when she thought she couldn't stand it any longer, he gave her what she craved. With a deep groan he lowered himself over her and she whispered his name again and again as he possessed her, carrying her far beyond the realms of ordinary pleasure into a timeless oblivion.

They must have slept afterwards, exhausted, limbs entwined, scarcely moving. Julia woke to find him watching her, the lines on his face miraculously erased, his hard mouth softened, incredibly tender. Her head was pillowed on his shoulder and his arm around her waist. Wonderingly, she raised a hand to his cheek, loving the rasp of his beard against her palm, not wanting to be in any other place.

'Don't leave me,' she implored suddenly, knowing she could never lose him now.

He kissed her several times before he answered, as though seeking to reassure her as he murmured teasingly, 'If I remember correctly, *ma mie*, you were planning to leave me. I never had any intention of leaving you. I love you too much.'

She still found it difficult to take in. 'Are you sure?'

'Yes.' The admission came rawly from his throat and a tremor ran through him.

'If only I'd known,' tears of regret stung her eyes, 'what a lot of bother it would have saved!'

'I would scarcely call it bother, *bien-aime*,' he told her wryly, then added so harshly that her eyes widened apprehensively, 'I was rough with you—I doubt if I shall ever forgive myself.'

'It was my fault,' she insisted. Hating to see his arrogance leaving him, even for a moment, she pressed her lips adoringly to his hard cheek. 'If I hadn't come here and planned to creep into your bed . . .'

'You really intended doing that?'

Because he was listening at last, she nodded. 'I'd planned to, but before I fell asleep I knew I wouldn't.'

'So,' his brow creased as he put a small space between them to gaze at her, 'what then?'

'I remember thinking I might just run away.'

'But not to André?'

'No,' she breathed painfully, 'but I have no proof.'

He looked deep into her beautiful eyes, his own worshipping. 'I believe you, *mignonne*,' he said slowly yet grimly, 'but do you believe me when I say Lorraine has been feeding you a lot of lies? I've never been her lover, or loved her.'

'Yes,' Julia was suddenly so sure she didn't hesitate, 'I trust you.'

'It seems we trust each other.' His face lightening perceptibly, he kissed her again. 'Which must be the ultimate test of true love.' Gathering her closer, he murmured thickly, 'I lost my head completely that night, something I'd never done before. You responded so ardently, I forgot it was the first time for you until it was too late. And I'm afraid,' he confessed, 'my regrets were shortlived. In fact, I welcomed what had happened as it gave me an excuse to insist you married me immediately.'

Colour crept adoringly under Julia's skin as she whispered, 'I'm glad you did, but I thought you'd married me only from a sense of honour, not because you loved me. Guy—' she paused uncertainly, 'I know we don't have to talk about Lorraine again, but there is one thing she said which still bothers me. She said you'd promised my father you would look after me.'

'No!' he denied curtly, but his face softened with understanding as Julia's went pale. Gently he caressed the colour back to her cheeks as he assured her, 'Again Lorraine could only have been guessing. I won't say I wouldn't have given your father such a promise, but he never asked me. Naturally he didn't anticipate dying so young, and he did make some kind of provision for you, even if it is taking a while to come through. No, it was simply because Mavis begged me to and I have a strong sense of family that I came to London to look you up.'

'Only that?'

He stared into her puzzled eyes as though he might

easily drown in them, then confessed tightly, 'I had
every intention of inviting you to live with us as you
were so young and Mavis wanted it. This I did, as you
well know, *ma chérie*, but as soon as I saw you I felt
extremely wary. I wasn't sure what it was, but
something about you appeared to threaten my hitherto
orderly existence. Why do you think,' his brows quirked
ironically, 'I was in such a hurry to marry you off? I
was acting, for the first time I could remember, without
total reason. After Pierre I gave up trying to get rid of
you, although I still refused to face the truth. Your
kisses,' his face darkened, 'were becoming like a wine I
couldn't do without, but even after I'd prevented you
from working for Léon, I wouldn't admit I loved you.'

'I felt the same way,' Julia admitted softly, her eyes
shyly meeting his. 'I knew I loved you more than Pierre
or André or anyone else, but I wouldn't face up to it
because I believed you were for Lorraine. That's why I
wanted to work for Léon and why I went out with
André. I was just trying to escape. When you wouldn't
let me and I realised it was too late, I decided crazily to
come here. I thought if I was found in your bed, you
would be so furious and disgusted you would throw me
out. I was going to borrow some money from you to
tide me over until I made some, and I imagined you
would be so eager to get rid of me you would agree.'

'Instead,' he groaned, 'it had the opposite effect.
Didn't you realise, *ma mie*, once I'd possessed you, you
could never have escaped? No force on earth could have
taken you from me.'

'Guy,' she whispered, shaken by the passion in his
voice, 'why were you so determined not to admit your
feelings?'

'I was afraid to,' he muttered. 'You were so young,
for one thing, and I was too old for you. I knew you
were attracted to me, but every time I kissed you I felt I
was taking advantage of your inexperience. Seeing you
with André nearly drove me wild, but that was what

made me acknowledge that I couldn't let you go. I think I came to l'Ejienne to fight one last battle with myself, but before I ever got here, if,' he smiled faintly, 'my small, concealed passenger had been able to read my thoughts, she would have known I'd already given in. I was going to return the next day and beg you to become my wife.'

'You wouldn't have needed to beg,' she cried, unable to bear seeing even a fleeting hint of vulnerability on his proud, dark face. 'I love you so much.'

'And I you,' he muttered thickly, his eyes devouring her, lingering so sensuously on her soft curves that she was immediately conscious of desire stirring again.

'Oh, darling,' she murmured helplessly, a sense of happiness and excitement making her eyes shine.

'That isn't a smug smile on your face, by any chance?' he exclaimed. Then, as she sobered instantly. 'Oh, *ma mie*, I was only teasing. I'm going to look after you for the rest of your life, and although it may sound trite, I'm going to make sure you never stop smiling.'

Her arms tightened round his neck, her heart beating so loudly she thought he must hear it. Because she just wanted to melt into him, she forced herself to say unsteadily, 'There's so much to talk about.'

'Later,' muttered Guy, his dominant side taking over again as he crushed her to him, and began making a sensuous assault on her mouth. 'All I need to know now is that you'll never stop loving me.'

Murmuring it again and again, Julia knew it was a promise she would always be able to keep, and as her body and mind became one with his, she knew she had reached one of the ultimate peaks of passion and contentment. The other might be when she bore his son, but that was for the future. And this she could face with supreme courage, knowing with certainty that their love would grow and flourish and that nothing could destroy it.

A WORD ABOUT THE AUTHOR

Margaret Pargeter was born in the quiet Northumbrian Valley, in the extreme northeast of England, where she lives today.

When did she first feel an urge to write? "Truthfully, I can't recall," she admits. "It must have been during my early teens. I remember carrying a notebook in my pocket, and while milking cows I would often take a break to scribble something down."

The jottings developed into short stories, and Margaret's first break came several years after she had married. Her husband talked her into entering a writing contest, and her work caught the eye of an editor, who asked her to write serial stories. From there she went on to complete her first romance novel, *Winds from the Sea* (Romance #1899).

Among the author's many blessings, which she likes to keep counting, is the "pleasure I get from knowing that people enjoy reading my books. And," she adds, "I hope they long continue to do so."

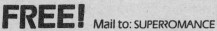